Mothers, Daughters, Wives

Short Stories & Poems

Dorothy Stewart

This edition published 2024 worldwide by Loaves & Fishes

Copyright © 2024 Dorothy Stewart

The right of Dorothy Stewart to be identified as the author of this work has been asserted in accordance with the Copyright, Designs & Patents Act 1988.

All rights reserved. No part of this publication may be reproduced, stored in a retrieval system, or transmitted in any form or by any means, electronic, mechanical, photocopying or otherwise, without the prior written permission of the publisher.

This is a work of fiction. Names, characters, places and incidents are either the product of the author's imagination or used fictitiously. Except where actual historical events and characters are being described for the storyline, all situations in this publication are fictitious and any resemblance to actual persons, living or dead, business establishments, events or locales is purely coincidental.

Cover design by Liz Carter

Contents

Introduction	5
1. Donkey Story	7
2. All That I Have…	13
3. The Girl He Left Behind	16
4. Roses Have Thorns	19
5. Raedwald's Queen	22
6. King of the Jews	25
7. One more stupid war	29
8. Happy Birthday, Mother!	31
9. Happy Christmas, Muriel	34
10. Practice Makes Perfect	42
11. Rhyme and Reason	46
12. Going On Holiday?	49
13. Hassan and the Lordly Ones	52
14. Balthazar's Feast	64
15. Homeward Bound	67
16. Rumours of Angels	69
17. Another Christmas on the Green	71
18. Here Be Dragons	74
19. Once Upon a Parking Space	77
20. MacAllister's Party: a story for Burns Night	83
Author's Notes	99

Introduction

I HAD A dream. Not the vision-type when you're wide awake, or the goal-setting ambitious one-DAY-I'll-do-this dream. No, a fast-asleep dream. In the dream I was driving my camper van (I haven't had one since the 1970s), setting off on a trip, an adventure.

And I found myself reversed into the kitchen of a motorway service station. The staff let themselves into the van by the side door and were going to restock the fridge. But when they opened it, it was still full of things from the previous trip. Salads in bags, still fresh enough to use, that sort of thing.

And it was clear that there was no way the staff were going to restock my fridge with nice new things until I emptied out and used up what was already in there.

When I woke, the dream was still fresh and vivid in my mind and when I poked around at it to see if I could work out what it meant, I realised it was referring to all the things I've written over the years – and done nothing with. I'd simply hidden them away.

Till now. I am emptying the fridge – and some of the contents I am sharing in this book are short stories and some of the hundreds of poems I've written, most of which have never seen the light of day before.

I hope you enjoy them – or at least find some that delight you. They are varied, some whimsical, some a little radical perhaps. Some are a fresh take on Gospel stories, some have Christmas as a linking theme, and others – perhaps the odder – can safely be considered odds and ends.

Which is a good way to end. And if you do enjoy them, perhaps you could take a moment to leave a review on Amazon or drop me a line at my blog:

https://www.dorothystewartblog.wordpress.com.

1. Donkey Story

There once was a man who had a wife and a donkey. The one was as gentle and affectionate as the other was obstinate and bad-tempered, but unfortunately for Simon, the first was his donkey and the second his wife.

Who would wonder then that he spent more time with the donkey, lingering in the warm stable even when he knew his supper was ready?

And his wife, knowing only too well where he was, would shout: 'Simon! Your food is ready. Are you still out there with that stupid, dirty animal?'

Both Simon and the donkey would prick up their ears as Tabitha's voice reached them – and everyone else in the village of Bethphage – and Simon would groan and stroke the donkey's head. She was his only comfort and he looked after her tenderly. No stick was ever raised against her, no one but Simon rode her or loaded her back. And his care was repaid beyond all measure when she gave birth to a perfect red-brown colt.

He proudly announced the news to Tabitha.

'Good!' she said. 'We can sell the colt and then...'

Simon paled. 'Sell the colt?'

'Easily,' Tabitha said. 'Only yesterday Mr Abrahams was saying he needed another donkey.'

'How dare you discuss *my* donkey with that man?' Simon said angrily. 'That donkey is *mine* and I am *not* going to sell the colt!'

Tabitha lost her temper. 'I don't understand you! All our life we've been poor – and it's all your fault! The way you've refused to be sensible and make money out of what we had. Oh no, you have to be *generous* and *help* other people, even it means giving things away! We could have had a comfortable life! And now, when at last we can get some money, you refuse! I warn you, Simon, I'm losing patience with you.'

'I will not sell the colt!' Simon repeated.

But Tabitha's anger worried him and he began to fear that she would steal the colt and sell it to Mr Abrahams. So now, instead of letting them run in the paddock after the day's work, he tied them to a ring in the doorpost and stationed himself against the wall nearby to guard them.

He had just finished tying them up one day when a stranger came by and stopped to stroke the colt's head.

'You have a fine animal here. Would you think of selling him?'

'Have you been talking to my wife?' Simon demanded. 'If she's said anything...'

'No, no! I simply saw the colt... So you won't sell?'

'No!'

'Would you perhaps lend him to someone who had need of him?'

Simon was by now annoyed both by the stranger and the topic. He said roughly, 'Look, mister, if you want to buy or borrow a colt, go somewhere else because this one is mine and he stays with his mother. I'm not selling him or lending him to anyone!'

The stranger looked at Simon and nodded, then walked on into the village.

Simon swore under his breath and kicked a stone into the gutter.

A soft chuckle startled him.

'Much better to sell to me, Simon my friend,' fat Mr Abrahams said. 'That's the prophet from Galilee. He's staying in Bethany and he hasn't any money to buy your colt. And if you loaned it to him, you'd never see it again. Sell the colt to me, Simon! You know my money's good.'

'No,' Simon growled. 'Never!'

Mr Abrahams waddled away, still chuckling.

Several months later the village was humming with news. The prophet from Galilee had done a great miracle at Bethany: he had raised a dead man to life. One man had seen Lazarus walk from the tomb in his grave clothes. Another had seen Lazarus a week later, full of vigour and praising God. There were lots of other stories too of the prophet's healings and teaching.

Simon, recalling his angry conversation with the stranger, felt uncomfortable. He was ashamed to have treated such a man, a prophet and a miracle-worker, so badly. It wasn't how he used to be...

And then it was the days before the feast of Passover, and Tabitha went into Jerusalem early to do some shopping. The atmosphere between them had gone from bad to worse and Simon was glad to be alone. He had often thought about the prophet and had finally decided that the man had come to him with a message from God, but his angry response had prevented the word from being spoken.

Simon led the donkey and the colt from the stable and tethered them to the ring in the doorpost. He was going to load them up for a day's work but just for a moment, he settled against the wall and looked at them gloomily. He wondered what the message would have been.

Two strangers approached and went straight to the donkeys, untying the animals.

'Hey!' Simon shouted, leaping up. 'What do you think you're doing?'

'The Lord has need of them,' one of the men replied.

The simple words stopped Simon in his tracks. 'The Lord?' Who could they mean? Then he remembered many thought this prophet from Galilee was someone special and called him 'Lord'. Simon's heart leapt, remembering the stranger's words: 'Would you perhaps lend him to someone who had need of him?' The prophet had not forgotten him! If he loaned him the donkeys, perhaps the prophet would return with them and give him the message from God!

Simon reached for the ropes to help the men. His hands faltered for a moment as he recalled Mr Abrahams saying 'If you loaned the colt to him, you might never see it again.' Then he pulled the rope free.

'Here,' he said, holding out the tethers. 'Please take them.'

Simon sat down against the wall and watched them walk away. For the first time in ages there was peace in his heart. He knew he had done the right thing. Warm in the sunshine, he fell asleep.

At dusk he awoke and looked towards the door for the donkeys. Then he remembered what he had done. How he had let them go. Panic struck him. Tabitha would never forgive him! She had been threatening to leave him... This would be the last straw for her. He shivered and bowed his head in despair.

A soft muzzle nuzzling him roused him. There by his side were the donkey and the colt. The prophet had sent them back. Rejoicing, Simon rose and hurried the two animals into the stable. Tabitha would never need to know!

'Simon! Simon!' Tabitha's impatient voice.

Simon smiled. Everything was back to normal. He stroked the donkey's muzzle and headed in for his supper.

But there was no supper.

'Are you all right?' he asked.

'I'm sorry, Simon. I've only just got home...'

'Trouble in town?'

'No,' she said. 'Not trouble...'

'So, what happened?'

'There was a procession!' she said excitedly. 'And I got caught up in it. It was wonderful!'

Her eyes shone.

'There were so many people, waving palm branches, throwing their robes on the road, dancing and singing 'Hosanna! Blessed is he that comes in the name of the Lord!' and then he came, riding into Jerusalem.'

'Who?'

'The Messiah, Simon! I have seen him with my own eyes! He's the prophet from Galilee, and he's the Messiah...'

'The Messiah... the prophet...' Simon's voice trailed away. The prophet who had sent the donkeys back but hadn't delivered his message...

'Yes!' Tabitha continued joyfully. 'He came riding like a king on a beautiful little colt with its mother trotting by its side. Oh, it was so wonderful... and I wept!'

'I thought you didn't like donkeys?' Simon said.

'Oh Simon, I'm so sorry...' Her tears spilled over. 'I realised how mean I've been – how your way of generosity and helping people is the right way, and my way of keeping everything to ourselves, trying to make money out of everything, was hard-hearted and unloving. And, Simon, I've been so unloving to you! I'm so sorry...'

Simon kissed her gently and took her hand.

'Come,' he said.

'Where?' she asked, bewildered.

'To the stable,' he said, pushing the door open. 'To the donkeys. You were looking at the Messiah so much you didn't recognise them.'

Then he told her his secret, about the prophet's word and the coming of the two men.

'You mean it was on *your* donkey that the Messiah rode into Jerusalem?'

Simon put his arms around her.

'No, my love, it was on *our* donkey.' And as Tabitha smiled back at him, Simon knew the Messiah had indeed passed on his message, to both of them.

2. All That I Have...

'**C**OME BACK HERE!'

'Oh Mum!'

'You're not twelve yet so you're still under my control,' Caleb's mother told him crossly. 'And you know what the Law says: Honour your mother and your father...'

Caleb muttered the words under his breath: Honour your mother and your father. He'd bet Moses wouldn't have put that one in if *his* mother had been a rotten cook.

'Right, there you are.' His mother handed over the food. 'And don't go getting into any trouble.'

'No, Mum,' Caleb headed quickly for the door, only to be stopped by 'And what do you say?'

'Thank you, Mum,' Caleb said obediently and made a fast exit.

His friend Aaron was waiting for him round the corner.

'I thought you'd never get away,' Aaron complained. 'What kept you?'

'Mum,' Caleb said. He gestured to the food container on his shoulder. 'I tried to get away but she insisted...'

'So what did she give you?' Aaron asked curiously.

'Some of her little barley loaves, and a couple of fish,' Caleb groused. 'And she knows I don't like fish.' He kicked a stone as far as he could get it. 'And I don't like her barley loaves either.'

Aaron prised himself off the ground where he'd been sitting waiting for Caleb.

'Don't worry,' he said. 'My Mum's given me some cheese and enough ripe figs to share. There will be plenty.'

'Good,' Caleb said, brightening up. 'Let's be going.' And the two friends set off for their day's adventure.

'What now?' Aaron asked, hours later. 'It's too early to go home.'

'I dunno,' Caleb said. They had spent the day by the shore of the lake, just messing around as boys do. Hot and tired and dirty, they were unwilling to go home while there was still light in the sky.

'What's going on over there?' Aaron pointed. Higher up on the grassy slopes of one of the hills, a crowd of people had gathered and were milling about.

'Dunno,' Caleb said, then taking to his heels and running toward the hill, he shouted back, 'But I'm going to find out! Are you coming?'

Aaron sped off and soon overtook him. Soon the two boys had arrived at the great grassy space, laughing and falling over each other in a mock fight.

'I got here first!'

'No, you didn't! I did!'

'Hush!' An unfamiliar grown-up voice.

Caleb and Aaron paused momentarily in their tussle.

'The Teacher may speak again,' the man who had spoken continued. 'Don't you want to hear him?'

The boys exchanged glances. Entertainers and magicians and miracle workers, wedding parties they could join in on, that was fun. But teaching? They got enough of that at school!

They exchanged quick glances and looked for an escape route, but everybody else was sitting down. Except for a small group of men who were talking quietly.

'Time to go,' Caleb whispered to Aaron and they began to move stealthily away. But the crowd seemed to shift and drift, and instead of getting away, Caleb and Aaron found themselves close to the men.

One said, 'Where can we buy enough bread for all these people?'

Caleb stared. Who could be rich enough to feed this huge crowd? There must be thousands of them there!

As if his thoughts had been heard, another man spoke up and said, 'It would cost a fortune just to give one little piece of bread to each one!'

'Exactly,' Caleb said out loud before he had thought.

'Well, what are we going to do?' the first man asked.

Caleb found himself tugging on the robe of the man nearest him.

'Excuse me.'

The man looked down and Caleb opened up the basket his mother had packed with food that morning. It was all still there. He had shared Aaron's cheese and figs and never touched the hated barley loaves and fish his mother had provided. This was a way of getting rid of them so he would not have to bring them home and face her wrath.

'Excuse me,' Caleb said. 'I know it's not much, but you can have these.'

3. The Girl He Left Behind

I KNEW HE would be going. He had told me, in so many ways. He came back from town one day. It was market day and he had gone with some of the farm animals to sell. He popped in to say hello and when he came to give me his customary hug, I knew. There was something wrong. I recoiled.

I don't think he noticed. There was a kind of tarnished glee about him. I didn't like it – or him – at that moment. And from then on, it went downhill, till at last he got his inheritance money from his father, packed his bags and left. Leaving me behind.

I had always felt there was an understanding between us… but nothing had been said, not by either one of us, or our parents. So after a few days of weeping, I had to put it behind me and get on with life.

Though I never stopped wondering. Who was it who had infected him with this wickedness? For infection it was. It wasn't who he really was!

I clung to that, despite what my mother said when she saw my red-rimmed eyes. 'He's not worth it.'

And my sisters: 'If he'd loved you at all, he wouldn't have gone.'

As the days went by, and then the weeks and months, the pain in my heart faded from sharp anguish to dull ache. But it never went away.

One day, slowly coming up the road, I noticed his father sitting on a large rock at the roadside, a little way away from the farm.

He nodded a polite greeting to my sisters and me. They giggled and whispered to one another. When we had passed by, something made me look back. The old man was simply sitting there, looking down the road.

'He does that every day,' Leah said. 'Watching for that useless boy come home. Complete waste of time, if you ask me.'

'Well, what else is he going to be doing, at his age?' Sarah replied. 'Might as well sit out here as get under people's feet back at the farm.'

I hurried to get my chores done then told my mother I'd like to just have a little walk in the cool by myself.

'Don't go too far,' she told me.

'I won't.' And I was gone like the wind, back to where the old man sat on his rock, motionless, eyes fixed on the long road. As I approached, I tried to walk quietly, but he didn't move.

I hunkered down on the ground beside the rock, facing down the road, just like him. That was the first day.

I came back every day after that, and just sat by his side. In a strange way, it eased the pain – we were doing something about our loss and hurt. Watching and waiting, though all the folk who went by shook their heads, even mocked. Because they did not believe he would come home.

But sitting there, each day, eyes fixed as far down the road as we could see, that was what we could do, to show our faith that God is good and God saves even the wretch who deliberately turns away and breaks the hearts of those who love him. And when you sit quiet, and wait on God, he gives you peace.

The old man never once queried my presence. Never asked my name. Never spoke to me. Till one day.

His voice quavering with excitement, he said, 'Your eyes are younger than mine, girl. Tell me, is that someone coming up the road towards us? Is that…'

And I was on my feet, tears pouring down my face.

'Yes! Yes!' I cried.

And then he was on his feet and running down the road! Yes, an old man like that, running down the road and flinging his arms round his son. His beloved son who had come home.

I watched a while, then went home. I needed to wash the tears from my face.

4. Roses Have Thorns

YOU DIDN'T KNOW he was married? What, the faithful son of Abraham who had obeyed every detail of the law since his youth? He wouldn't overlook the condemnation of the rabbis on the Jew who remains without a wife! And he wouldn't have married just anyone. Oh, no! (And maybe that was his mistake.) He had to marry someone who could trace her lineage back to the beginning. A daughter of Abraham, but more: a daughter of Levi, a daughter of the Temple. At the beginning, it got him lots of advantage. He was well pleased with his bargain...

What was he like as a husband? Well, you know Saul. He never did anything by halves! We were going to have the marriage that surpassed even the Song of Songs! He recited that book so often – at appropriate times, if you understand me! I think I could recite it myself from start to finish.

Children? Yes. I gave him sons and daughters. What was he like as a father? He could be harsh, when he saw them doing wrong. You see, that was his nature: a Godfearing Jew who desired to be perfect in the Law and please Jehovah. That's why he was sometimes harsh with the boys. (Never the girls – they could wind him round their fingers!)

It was about honour – the honour of the family. As a teacher of the law, it was necessary that his household held to the highest standards so when the boys did something that he felt brought dishonour to the house, he beat them. 'Spare the rod and the child will be spoiled' he'd quote from the book of Proverbs. But at heart he was a good, loving man. A happy family man, I'd have said. Until that business with the Nazarene.

When the followers of this Nazarene, Jesus, starting teaching in the Temple and telling people that he was the Messiah – this man who was tried before the Sanhedrin and judged a false prophet by the High Priest himself! A man crucified by the Romans as a rabble-rouser! Well, my husband couldn't just let that go on unopposed. It was the honour of the Jews and Jehovah at stake.

Of course, I supported him. You can't let these things get out of hand – especially when the Romans were always looking for an excuse to crack down on our people. They'd have loved a riot!

And off Saul went. I was so proud of him. He actually volunteered to go to Damascus and sort out the heretics there. But something happened. Something very strange, and he came back... different.

Well, you always think it's got to be another woman, don't you? There was that shine about him... that distracted air. It was clear to me that he was in love. We had quite a row about that!

Everybody knows now that it was Jesus. Dead though Jesus was, he changed all our lives. Saul became Paul and off he went. .. here, there and everywhere, preaching this new gospel. And we stayed here. The children were grown and married but it was an embarrassment to them. And me? A daughter of Levi? I was his big failure. I never converted to his new faith. Oh, he treated me fairly, saw that I was provided for and sent regular letters so I knew where he was and what he was doing. (Very good at writing letters, he was.)

I was sorry when he ended up in prison in Rome. I knew it would end badly. That sort of thing always does.

My name? Rose. 'I am a rose of Sharon' as the Song of Songs says. Ah, how he used to whisper to me from that lovely book. Latterly, of course, I wasn't his beloved Rose. No, I was the thorn, begging him to come home, to give up his mad love affair with this Jesus and his crazy journeys.

It's no compliment to be called a thorn – but it is some comfort to know he never forgot me.

5. Raedwald's Queen

I am the nameless one, like so many before me
and, sadly, after. Yet I had power –
real power and influence over my king.
The closeness of the marriage bed
can win more than sons for a clever woman,
and I was clever – until he came home from Kent,
baptised in the new faith. I raged –
no better than the raw-handed fisher-girls
screaming like gulls at their drunken sots of husbands.
I raged. I railed. But he would not give way.
I built my arguments: this would split our people,
weaken his rule.
But still he held to his new God – this Christ
from across the sea.
I turned my back on him, despite my longing,
and he made an uneasy truce. The altar
to his new God
would not replace our old one but sit, side by side.

At last, I went into his arms. But it was like
a rotting tooth,
this dissension between us, where before there
was only joy.

Then he took the wound that took him,
finally, from me,
and I, holding fast to my own faith
and the faith of the people,
built him a fitting monument –
his beloved ship beneath him,
a fine chamber upon it, and all he needed
for the next life,
all of the finest, lavished there.
But at the last I faltered.
I had trusted my lord in all but this –
what if he were right?
What if this new God did indeed eclipse the old gods?
No Valhalla feasting awaiting my lord, but the risen
hand-piercèd Christ?
So I took the silver baptismal spoons, engraved with
foreign names – Saulus, Paulus –
and I placed them close, where the Christ
would see them.
Some fine bowls, engraved with the Christian cross,
I laid these near.
And when all was done, the mound covering
him over,
the feasting finished to the last drops,
the people gone,

I laid my cheek against the side and whispered to him,
my lord and my love,
what I had done. Just in case he had been right. His
new faith the true one.
And I heard him chuckle, as he always did when he
won a game against me.
Aye, the best man wins, he answered me, as always.
And at last,
I could weep for him, and for me, and for our people,
and all the changes that were coming, Gods and all.

6. King of the Jews

I CAME TO see a man killed today. Yes, I knew crucifixion was an ugly way to die, but I wanted to see him die, to see him dead. Maybe then we could be at peace.

I had gone with the crowds to watch him carry his cross up the hill. I was prepared for the wait, however long it took, however horrible. I wanted to see him dead. Gone. Finished. Maybe then I could find peace.

I laughed when I saw the crown they had given him, this King of the Jews – a crown of thorns! We've been a thorn in the flesh of many who tried to rule us. None have succeeded. And he hadn't even tried. Fine king he was.

I scuffed the road at my feet in disgust. We had needed a king, needed a leader to get us out from under the Romans – Gentiles polluting our land.

It had seemed possible. When word went round of the man from Galilee, when we heard of the things he did… My brother and his friends got very excited.

'Don't you see, Adina! It's all coming true, the prophecies about the Messiah!'

My father tried to quieten him. 'Many have come that we thought – that we hoped – would be the Messiah.'

'But no one has done the miracles this man has done,' my brother protested. 'The blind see, the lame walk, the lepers are cured, the deaf hear, and the dead are raised to life! This man is the Messiah, my father, and we must rise up against the Romans and bring in his kingdom!'

My mother's eyes were fearful as she listened to this wild talk. But that was nothing to the chill in our hearts when we learnt that my brother and his friends had been arrested, caught in a wild hardly planned attack on the Roman barracks on the outskirts of our village. Caught, arrested – and crucified.

I had seen my brother die, and now I wanted to see this man die, this man my brother had said was the Messiah, this man who had turned out to be just one more false prophet.

I kicked the stones at my feet savagely. I'd had enough of Messiahs, enough of false prophets, even Moses himself. It was all false, all in vain, mad ideas that drove silly, idealistic boys to wildness and death.

I hated this false Messiah who had caused my brother's death. And now it was his turn. Now, he too would die. And that would be the end of it.

He stumbled up the hill, the massive cross bar crushing his shoulders, beads of blood like berries among the thorns that made his crown. Sweat poured from him, sweat mingling with blood and dust. He stumbled, and I almost – *almost* – felt sorry for him. Just another man on his way to die. But I hardened my heart, reminded myself that I hated him, hated what he had done to my family. We would never be the same.

Crowds lined the way. Some people shook their fists at him. Others jeered and shouted abuse. Some spat.

As he drew closer, he staggered, then fell on his knees under the weight of that terrible burden. His arm came up to brush the sweat and blood from his eyes.

I looked upon him, this Messiah, this King of the Jews. He turned his head and looked at me. His eyes seemed to plead with me. For a long, frozen moment, I stood rooted to the ground.

A movement at my side woke me. Pushing past me, a young girl of about my own age, slender, blushing with embarrassment but determined. She stepped out on the road, her veil torn from her head outstretched in her hand.

The man took it from her and mopped his face. He handed it back to her, his eyes gentle and warm. She smiled a brief moment, then tears filled her eyes as she turned and fled back into the crowd.

His eyes followed her, then turned back to me. I could not hold his gaze, and dropped my eyes. I could not bear for him to look upon me with those eyes of gentleness.

With an effort, he rose from the ground and, shouldering his cross once more, began the ascent again to Calvary.

I did not follow. The crowd flowed around me, but I stayed. I could not move. Those eyes had touched my very depths.

I knew this man was not the Messiah my brother and his friends had looked for. He was not one who would overcome the Romans with sword and spear and wild boys spoiling for a fight.

No, he was not that kind of King of the Jews. But in his eyes I saw his kingliness. In his eyes, I saw a glimpse of his kingdom, and that was higher, wider, greater far than the little kingdom my brother and his friends had been willing to die for.

Yet I had not even been willing to offer him my veil to wipe his face. The moment had come, and passed. And I knew, with a terrible certainty, that this man was indeed the promised Messiah. This man was indeed the King of the Jews. And up on that hill, they were crucifying him.

I had looked for an end, for peace. But there would not be an end. And how could there be peace for those like me who turned away from him?

7. One more stupid war

I have his letters –
the youngest of the great-uncles,
Danny,
a boy-name for a beloved brother –
wrapped in soft, rough brown paper,
pencil-written notes
from a hand more used to sowing and planting,
tending crops and animals,
than writing to his mother.
The censor's pen has slashed through the place-names
'Somewhere in France'
and that's where his body lies,
in the mud and screaming carnage
of one more stupid war.
And thousands of miles away
the bog cotton waves white pompoms of peace
over the deserted croft
and the long northern sky looks down.

And another boy dies screaming in a foreign land
in an even more meaningless war,
while the warlords,
this time in business suits not khaki uniforms,
count the value of their shares in oil.

8. Happy Birthday, Mother!

My mobile rang as I was leaving the house. In far too much of a hurry, I ignored it and flung my bag with the mobile in it onto the passenger seat of the car, did up my seat belt and roared away from the house. If the traffic wasn't too heavy, I might just get to work on time.

At the office, my handbag was shoved into the bottom drawer of my desk and the happenings of the day avalanched on top of me – as always. So I didn't get time to check who had phoned me until lunchtime. Or rather, on the way back to work after lunch.

I was in the lift when I remembered so I rummaged in my bag, found my mobile and accessed the Answer service. As I stepped out of the lift into the corridor, I could hear that, as expected, I had one new message. I pressed to listen, then as the voice came through loud and clear and complaining, I turned my face to the wall so no one could see the tears start.

My mother. She had received the flowers I had sent for her birthday. Very nice. She realised I was busy. Hadn't had time to pick out something more personal – like my sister had. *She* had sent the most exquisite blouse. It would match her new jacket perfectly. She was so fortunate in having such a thoughtful daughter. Didn't I think perhaps I should slacken up a bit? Give some time to my family? The mother who had done so much for me? Perhaps even find time to visit on her birthday?

Well, yes, I am busy. Unlike my sister, I work full-time. I had been away on a business trip and hadn't had time to shop around for something perfect for Mum's birthday. Not that it's possible for me to get anything perfect. It's my job to get it wrong so my sister can be perfect and get it right. It's always a competition, and one I'm getting pretty tired of. Not as tired as with the guilt trips, though.

I shook myself. Stop that. She's a lonely old lady and if sniping at me kept her going then surely I had broad enough shoulders to cope. Yeah, sure, but inside there was still the little girl who could never get anything right – and it still hurt.

Someone was coming towards me so I switched the mobile off, squared my shoulders, fixed a bright competent smile on my face and headed back into work. What Mum didn't know was that I was going to visit her this evening. And even more unusual, my sister and I would be going together. If I could face her after my devastating defeat on the presents stakes, that is.

The day flew by, as always, and I was in the usual rush to get my car and fight the going-home traffic. I was running ten minutes late when I rang my sister's doorbell. Inside was the sound of yelling. Oh-oh. Life with kids.

The door opened and not for the first time I decided that women should have been designed with more than one pair of hands. My sister was trying to hold the door open, fight off the dog, struggle into her coat, and at the same time as greeting me, was trying to make her instructions to her two kids heard above the barking.

She was also fumbling with her mobile. As she put it to her ear, I realised she'd mistakenly pressed the loudspeaker button as I could hear quite clearly. It was our mother. She had received Janet's present. A blouse. Very nice. Really. She realised that Janet was probably too busy with her own family now to spend much time on her mother who had done so much for her. Not like her younger sister who had gone to the trouble of picking out a beautiful bouquet of the most exquisite flowers…

Janet went bright red and there were tears in her eyes as she stabbed at her mobile to silence it. I held out mine, and pressed the loudspeaker button so she could hear Mum's message to me.

As she listened, her eyes widened. By the time we heard Mum out, we were giggling. We looked at each other and the giggles became chortles. Janet held out her arms to me and we clutched at each other in a hug that buckled and bounced with laughter and tears.

'Wonderful,' she said, wiping her eyes.

'Mum.' It was her teenage son. 'What's going on?'

We looked at each other and Janet grinned at me.

'It's a sister thing,' she told him.

9. Happy Christmas, Muriel

Mrs Muriel Strachan (pronounced Strawn) adjusted her hat on the crisp white curls of her freshly permed hair and permitted herself a nod of approval.

'Very nice,' she told the girl who had done her hair.

'Have a lovely Christmas,' Julie replied with a warm smile.

Muriel's mouth clamped tight and the carefully manicured fingers counting out change for the tip stilled. The last few coins slid back into the recesses of her purse and Muriel snapped it shut. She dropped the coins she had removed into the saucer with its 'Thanks ever so!' label, then drew on her gloves.

'Put me down for my usual next week,' she instructed the girl. 'I suppose you will be open?'

'Oh yes, Mrs Strachan,' Julie whispered, chastened, as she turned the long pages of the salon diary. 'Friday, half past three, as usual?'

'Of course.'

And after seeing it was entered in the book, she gave the girl a frosty nod and sailed grandly into the shopping mall.

'What did I do wrong, Maggie?' the girl wailed to her friend and colleague. 'I only wished her a happy Christmas ...'

'Probably a bit too personal, love. She doesn't like that. But don't you worry. She'll have forgotten by the time she comes back.'

But Muriel had not forgotten. 'Lovely Christmas indeed!' she muttered to herself as she made her statuesque way through the busy throng of Christmas shoppers. What was the use of that? She had no time for Christmas, all alone now that Jim was dead – not that he was ever much use. If only Philip had not been such a delicate child. Who knew what he might have achieved. He'd have been a comfort to his mother in her old age, that was sure.

'Muriel!' Edna Alexander's piercing voice jolted her out of her thoughts. She found she was standing, staring blindly into the window of a large toyshop. To her horror, there were tears in her eyes. In the window's reflection she could see Edna bearing down on her from the other side of the mall. Suddenly she could not bear Edna's company even though they always met for tea and a 'putting the world to rights' session on a Friday afternoon. Now, all she wanted was to be alone but there seemed no escape... except inside the toyshop.

It was years since Muriel had been in a toyshop. That last gift had been for Philip when he was in hospital, now lovingly displayed with all his other toys in his bedroom at home. Morbid, that's what Jim called it, but Muriel found it comforting, even after all this time.

Inside the toyshop was worse than she could have guessed from the window display. And the noise! Bewildered, she gazed at robots and computer games consoles. Nothing seemed the same. Where were the teddy bears and soft toys that Philip had loved?

A hasty exit seemed the best idea but as she turned to leave, she spotted Edna peering into the shop. Just in time, Muriel ducked behind a towering pile of boxes on special offer and collided with an assistant, a middle-aged man wearing a stern expression.

'Can I help you, madam?'

'No! I mean, yes! I mean...' Muriel was furious to find she was stammering.

'Can't find the right gift?' the man suggested.

Muriel took a surreptitious peek behind her. Edna was still visible. Why wouldn't she go away and leave her alone?

'Yes, that's right!' Muriel gave in. 'It's all so different...'

'Well, times change, don't they?' The man smiled with satisfaction. 'All our gifts are right at the leading edge....'

'Well, I was looking for something a little more...'

'Traditional?' The man was frowning. 'What age is the child in question?'

Muriel thought frantically. Philip had been nearly three when he died.

'Three!' she declared triumphantly.

'Soft toys, then,' the man said, sounding disappointed and led the way to the back of the store. There, heaped on shelf above shelf, was every colour and size of creature imaginable – gorillas, penguins, dragons, turtles, and lots of different kinds of dinosaurs.

'A teddy bear?' Muriel faltered.

'Teddy bear.' The man sighed and turned down another aisle. At the end was an untidy mountain of teddy bears: dark fur, golden fur, pink and blue fur, large, medium and small teddy bears, all higgledy-piggledy and just begging to be cuddled.

'I'm sure you'll be able to find what you're looking for here,' the man told her.

Muriel began rummaging among the teddy bears, waiting for the man to leave and give her a chance to escape. But he started pulling teddy bears out of the heap and presenting them to her.

'What about this one? Or this?'

Gritting her teeth, Muriel chose a small teddy bear with golden fur and shining amber eyes.

'This one,' she said. A small price to pay to get away from this stupid situation. If only Edna Alexander had not spotted her!

Muriel paused before leaving the shop. Even though the teddy bear was wrapped in garish Christmas paper, with a huge ribbon bow and a loop for carrying it, it was still only too recognisably a teddy bear. She looked to the left and right, and left again as if she were carefully crossing a road. Good! No sign of Edna. Perhaps she would be able to get her shopping done without Edna spotting her.

Loudspeakers piped tinny Christmas carols into the air, competing with a small group of singers, one of the members shaking a collecting tin hopefully. Muriel bristled and hurried past them. At the supermarket, she stuffed the teddy bear out of sight beside her handbag in the bottom of the trolley and consulted her list. There! That should do. As she packed the food into carrier bags, she nearly forgot the teddy bear, sitting alone in the trolley.

'Don't forget your teddy bear!' the woman on the checkout called out to her. 'Present for a grandchild is it?'

The woman's cheerful smile faded at the fury on Muriel's face. Couldn't she mind her own business? She'd have to get rid of the teddy bear as soon as possible, but as she left the supermarket, Edna Alexander's voice reached her once again.

'Cooee! Muriel! Over here!'

Right, Muriel thought. I'll go the other way. I don't want her to catch me with this... thing! She couldn't bear having to explain why she had bought it. She wasn't too sure she really knew anyway. Muriel ducked through a set of swing doors and found herself abruptly outside, in the cold and dark of the late winter afternoon. It was a service road for the shopping mall, lined with lock-up garages. Large wheelie bins from the shops and cafes inside the precinct stood in an untidy row, spilling their smelly contents in heaps on the ground. The few streetlamps cast strange shadows, making Muriel hesitate.

But Edna was back in there. There could be no going back. Muriel swallowed hard and started out with as firm a step as she could manage, the teddy bear grasped tightly in her hand. A sudden movement in the shadows made her swing round, startled and fearful. A drunk or a rough sleeper, she thought. If only she could get away... How ever had she got into this predicament?

'What's your problem?' a voice challenged her.

It was a girl, young with long hair tangled and dirty, her face thin and bitter.

Muriel made to move on quickly, drawing her coat closer round her. The girl was probably a drug addict. Maybe even a mugger. She grasped her handbag more firmly and turned away. Then a tiny whimper of sound made her turn back and stare. The girl was adjusting her thin coat and Muriel could see, in the glow of the streetlights, the sleepy face of a baby. The girl wrapped herself round the child protectively.

'What you staring at?' she snarled. 'Never seen a baby before?'

'Well, yes, actually,' Muriel found herself saying. 'I had a child myself. He was called Philip. But he died. He was only – nearly three.'

'I'm sorry,' the girl said. 'I didn't mean...'

Embarrassed by the compassion in the girl's eyes, Muriel tore the teddy bear from its wrappings and thrust it at her.

'Here! Have this, for the baby. For Christmas. It's a Christmas present.'

It was a long time since she'd given anyone a Christmas present. A long time since she'd bothered with Christmas. She remembered the little hairdresser's 'Have a lovely Christmas' and her own hostile reaction. It was such a very long time since she'd had a lovely Christmas. Back when Philip was alive and well and there seemed to be so many reasons for living.

'A Christmas present?' the girl said slowly. 'For the baby? But isn't it for someone you know? You can't just give it to a stranger.' The girl peered at her. 'You some kind of a nutter?'

And Muriel, thinking of her warm house with its spare bedroom turned into a shrine for the little boy who hadn't come home from hospital thirty years ago while today this girl and her baby shivered amongst the rubbish bins at Christmas, decided she probably had been, locking out all the good things of life and hanging on to her grief. But maybe it wasn't too late.

She took a deep breath and plunged in.

'Have you anywhere to go?' she asked the girl.

'I've got here!' the girl threw back defiantly.

'Here?' Muriel said. 'This is no place for a baby!'

'I know that!' the girl screamed at her, tears streaming down her face. 'I wouldn't be here if I'd anywhere else to go but my boyfriend threw us out, my stepdad won't have us in the house, my Mum won't talk to me, the hostels are full, and I can't afford bed and breakfast or anywhere else!' The girl turned away and wept.

Muriel reached out and touched her shoulder hesitantly. 'I've got a spare room,' she said. 'If you'd like that...'

'You?'

Muriel nodded. 'I kept it for my little boy – but he doesn't need it any more.' (And maybe neither do I, Muriel thought.) 'And I'd be happy for you to have it. What do you say? It would tide you over.'

'Are you sure?' the girl asked. 'You don't know me...'

'I'm sure,' Muriel said and discovered she was holding her breath, hoping so hard...

'Well, thank you...'

Muriel overruled her hesitant thanks with brisk organisation. 'We'll need to get some more food... Christmas things, turkey, mince pies. You like those?' and like a whirlwind she gathered up the girl and the baby and their few things, tucked the teddy bear safely in the child's hands and bore them off back to the shopping mall and into the supermarket, talking all the way. 'And I'm sure if I rang your mother...'

'Muriel! Cooee!' Edna Alexander's voice was petulant.

'Can't stop now, Edna!' Muriel called back with a cheery wave. 'Got some friends staying for Christmas! Happy Christmas, Edna!' and as she piled the trolley high with brussels sprouts and cranberry sauce and Christmas pudding and brandy butter ('You do like brandy butter?') and all the other Christmas treats she could think of, her face began to shine with happiness.

The little hairdresser coming out of work late saw the two women and the baby with their overflowing bags of shopping struggling into a taxi.

'Maggie!' she whispered, 'that looks like Mrs Strachan. But she's smiling…'

'No way, Julie! I've never seen her smile, have you?'

10. Practice Makes Perfect

✤

I WAS ELEVEN when I decided that I wanted to be an angel when I grew up. I'd seen the leather-clad couriers tearing around town on their powerful motorbikes and the skinny people in Lycra with their strange speed helmets and racing bikes. But I knew that the best kind of messenger – the kind I wanted to be – was the kind with wings and robes of dazzling white. The angel kind, who suddenly appear with a special message and then vanish again. Yes. I wanted to be angel. It sounded just the job for me.

There was a girl called Mary who went to my school. She lived in the next street to me so, since it was that time of year, I thought I'd pop round to her house and practise. I have to admit that tripping over my long white robes as I got off my bike just outside her window didn't make an impressive start, and I was sure that angels were meant to be impressive.

I was determined to do this properly. That's why I'd found the nice clean white sheet in the airing cupboard to wrap around me and hide my school uniform. Well, it was nice and white and clean when I started out. It was a pity about the muddy puddle that I'd splashed through.

Once I'd disentangled the sheet from my bike, I rearranged it carefully so the folds hid the dirty bits. Then I rang Mary's doorbell and took a deep breath.

'Hail, O favoured one!' I announced when she came to the door.

I was satisfied to see that stopped her in her tracks. But only for a moment.

'Oh, it's Johnny Gabriel. What do you want?'

That threw me. She didn't seem the slightest bit worried and that meant the next bit didn't sound right: 'Do not be afraid, Mary'. But I was determined to say my piece, all of it, properly, even if she had gone back into the house.

So I followed her in and found her lolling on the sofa in front of the television.

'Do not be afraid, Mary,' I said in a loud enough voice to carry over the noise of the television. 'For you have found favour with God. And behold, you will conceive in your womb and bear a son, and you shall call his name Jesus!'

Whew! I'd said it and got all the words right and in the right places. Pleased with this success, I opened my eyes which I'd been keeping tightly shut to help me concentrate. I'd copied the words out of my Mum's Bible and it had taken days to learn them off by heart. Now I wanted to see the effect of the announcement.

I had seen lots of pictures of Mary and the angel. Usually she was kneeling with her hands clasped and a kind of glow round her head. Her eyes were big and blue and she was always gazing up at the angel in a soppy kind of way. (I liked that.) And the angel was always standing proudly tall in his long white robes. (I liked that too.) I pulled myself up to my full height and arranged my face into the kind of kindly-angel look I'd seen in the pictures.

But where was Mary? Instead of kneeling and gazing up at me the way I expected, she was curled up in a tight ball on the sofa and crying! This wasn't how it was meant to be! None of the Marys in the pictures were shown doing that! But this Mary seemed in a terrible state.

Her face was red and scrunched up. Tears were pouring down her face and her hands – there was no sign of beautiful white hands stretched out in prayer. Instead, her red fists were stuffed into her mouth stifling terrible noises like sobs. Now what was I supposed to do?

I stared at her in horror, frozen to the spot. Then I racked my brains for something to say but all I could remember were the words I'd learnt. Maybe now the opening words seemed more sensible.

'Do not fear, Mary,' I began, rather desperately this time, 'for you have found favour...'

And that's when her mother appeared. She had been taking her coat off and changing from her work clothes when I arrived. I suppose I'd expected her to be in the kitchen or somewhere, but here she was, advancing on me.

I backed away. I didn't like the look in her eye. This wasn't supposed to happen. Angels are supposed to be listened to with due respect. And there wasn't anything in the Bible about Mary's Mum getting involved at this stage, was there?

But *this* Mary's Mum was right here and getting closer, so I got out of her way. Fast. But she headed past me as if I wasn't there and went straight to the sofa. In one fast move, she reached down and enfolded Mary in her arms, and then she rocked her gently backwards and forwards. That was when

Mary took her clenched hands out of her mouth to return her mother's hug and I could see her face clearly.

Those terrible noises had not been sobs. They'd been laughter. Hysterical laughter. She hadn't been *crying* at all. Well, tears had been pouring down her face but not because she was scared or upset. She had been laughing so much she had been crying with laughter. And now her Mum was at it too.

'Oh, you daft boy!' her Mum managed to say, wiping her eyes. 'You're only a couple of thousand years too late!'

Well, I knew that. But, like I said, if I'm going to be an angel when I grow up, I've got to practise.

11. Rhyme and Reason

✥

'Well, I don't think it's funny.'

The first voice was a bit rusty, maybe not used to being used that much.

The second voice was a lot younger. 'You've got no sense of humour, that's your problem.'

'I like to say things as I find them,' the first voice insisted. 'And I say they don't wear socks.'

The announcement was met with silence, so the first speaker repeated: 'No socks. Dirty feet in dirty sandals. You've got to get it right.'

'Well, all right,' the second voice said. 'But it wouldn't rhyme.'

'Humph!' first voice snorted. 'Rhyme, fal-de-lals, artistic nonsense.'

'Do you call a sky full of angels artistic nonsense?'

'Ah. There you have me. I must say He can put on a good show.' First voice sighed with loud contentment. 'And that was a good show. Glorious. *Glory…*'

'Don't sing!' second voice said quickly, urgently.

'Oh, don't worry. Nobody pays any heed to sheep. Off they went to Bethlehem, to see the new-born king, leaving us behind...'

The old sheep gave a croaking noise, a rusty kind of laugh. 'And we got the best concert in the whole world: a sky full of angels singing to us!'

'I thought you said nobody pays any heed to sheep?' the younger one demanded crossly.

'Ah well,' the old sheep said. 'I meant people. There are people who think they're important, and they boss around the people they think aren't important, and they boss around the people further down... and so on, down to the people and the animals – like sheep – that they think don't matter at all. But what happened that night changed everything. A king born in a stable not a palace! Sending for a bunch of dirty shepherds *not wearing socks* to pay homage. And a sky full of angels serenading a hillside full of sheep. Not at all what was expected!'

'So why do it that way?' the youngest sheep asked. 'When everybody was expecting something different?'

'Because that's what He's like – God, I mean,' the old sheep said. 'He does things His way. And that's not the way of the high-ups and the powerful on earth. He's a God who notices the little people and cares about them.'

'And us?' the youngest sheep asked.

'And us,' the old sheep agreed. 'That's why He's called the Good Shepherd and he sent His own very special little lamb to us that first Christmas.'

'So it's logical He'd want shepherds there.'

'With no socks,' came the sharp reminder.

'Do you think God wears socks?' a small persistent voice asked.

'Don't be silly!' the older sheep said. 'Whoever heard of a God wearing socks!' There was a thoughtful pause. 'But He did wear nappies, when He came to Earth as a baby… like any other human baby.' The old sheep shook its woolly head. 'Amazing, when you think of it. A God who was willing to wear nappies!'

12. Going On Holiday?

❖

THE QUEUE SNAKED almost out of the bank door. Mel peered in. The place was jammed solid. There were harassed mothers with fractious toddlers. Groups of gossiping girls laden with shopping. Wobbly elderly people on sticks. Impatient businessmen checking watches and drumming their fingers. And the three young women at the cashiers' till windows were struggling to cope.

Mel took his place at the end of the queue, grateful for a place inside. Outside, the sky was heavy and beginning to get dark. Rain was falling in great fat drops. No wonder the Foreign Exchange counter was so busy. Everyone wanted to go abroad for the holiday.

With snail-like slowness the queue crawled forward taking Mel with it and at last, he found himself at the front. The man ahead of him at the Foreign Exchange counter seemed to be doing something very complicated. Bags of currency were mounding up on the counter and finally an enormous heap of travellers cheques. The man stuffed the money bags into a huge satchel. The travellers cheques he wrapped in waxed cloth and tied carefully, before stowing the bulky package away. His fat greasy face gleamed as he turned with a satisfied smile from the counter. Then the tiny black eyes snapped and two strapping youths stepped forward to escort him from the bank.

'I'm not surprised,' Mel thought as he took his place at the recently vacated counter.

'Yes, sir?' the teller enquired.

'Travellers cheques,' Mel began. 'I haven't ordered any but…'

'I'm terribly sorry.' The teller waved her hands apologetically. 'We've none left. There's been such a run on them today and now that last customer has cleaned me out completely.'

'No travellers cheques?' Mel said incredulously. 'But you can't! I need them most urgently. I'm travelling tomorrow.'

'I'm sorry, sir,' the teller repeated. 'At this time of year, there's no chance that we will have any more travellers cheques – for at least a couple of weeks. We have to order them, you see.'

'A couple of weeks!' Mel was appalled. 'That's no good to me at all. I need them today.'

'Perhaps we could let you have the appropriate currency instead?' the teller suggested.

'That wouldn't do,' Mel told her gloomily. 'The thing is I'm not sure what I'd need.'

'Make a guess – on the generous side,' the teller said brightly. 'Then you'll have enough!'

'No, that's not what I mean.' Mel said. 'What I mean is I don't know what kind of currency I'm going to need. That's why I thought travellers cheques…'

The teller's tired face briefly showed interest. 'A mystery trip?' she asked.

'Something like that.'

'I'm really sorry,' she said. 'With no travellers cheques left, I can't see how I can help you.'

A nudge in his back reminded Mel of the queue behind him.

'Okay, okay,' he said wearily and pushed his way out of the bank and into the rainy night.

Shop lights glittered, selling food and toys and party clothes, wine and jewellery, watches and gold chains....

Mel paused. Gold. That was an international currency. He looked up. The star was shining brightly in the now dark sky. Melchior plunged into the jewellery store to change his savings into gold for the journey, gold for the king.

13. Hassan and the Lordly Ones

✺

Hassan lolled in the shade of his mother's tent and dreamed. He dreamed of when he'd be old enough to ride out with the men on the fleetest of camels, scimitars flashing in the sun, as they raided the tents of their enemies. In his dreams, he was a hero, a man of valour. Great would be the booty he would return with.

The shadow lengthened and darkened. Hassan stared up into strange dark eyes. A scimitar flashed close to his throat and fear surged in his blood. The man laughed. Hassan felt hatred – and terror. All around were screams, and terrible sights.

The man seized him by the neck of his burnous and hauled him to his feet. Then he dragged him out of the shade and safety of the tent and into the burning sun where there was terror and blood. Hassan hid his eyes so he would not see the full horror as he was dragged past the tents of his people.

Bound and tied to a camel, for all the world like a roll of carpet, he thought disgustedly. He spat out the sand from his mouth and with it a whispered curse for the raiders who had murdered his mother and his kin while the menfolk were away. One day he would have his revenge! One day when he was grown....

The Lordly Ones

HASSAN, THE CAMEL-boy, watched the strangers ride into the courtyard of the inn. They were finely dressed, and their camels were richly decked, the harness sparkling and jingling in the morning sunlight. He came running from the stable to help them dismount and was pleased to find a gold coin pressed into his hand as reward.

'Mind you tend our camels well!' one of the men commanded him. Hassan bowed low. He much preferred rich travellers who paid him generously, so he led the camels away and unloaded them carefully, stacking the heavy saddlebags together. The dust and travel-stains showed they and their lordly riders had been on the road many days.

Hassan remembered the long days of the painful journey that had taken him from his home. Pain etched in his face as he recalled the brutality of the raiders and the humiliating slave auction at the end of the caravan route. Then he shrugged his shoulders. He had been very small when the raiders had come and he had been quite lucky, considering.

His master, fat Johab, the innkeeper was not a bad man and Hassan had got used to working within the confines of the inn, clearing the empty tankards off the tables. He had a warm place by the fire to sleep at night and plenty of food. And gradually, as he'd proved himself trustworthy and unlikely to run away, he had been given the job of looking after the stables.

When he had settled the camels, brushed them down, and fed and watered them, Hassan crept into the inn to take another look at these lordly men. They looked rich, and they sounded rich and powerful. One was standing by the fire, telling everyone in the room that they were on a grand quest.

'We have come many miles to find a king, a newly born king,' the man said, looking around the room at the interested faces. 'What news do you have of him?'

The other men in the room shook their heads and murmured that they knew nothing. 'Haven't heard a thing!'

The three men shook their heads disgustedly. 'We'll wait till nightfall, then we can get on the road again,' one of the men said to his companions.

The other people in the room laughed loud and long at this. The nights were dark and there was no moon. The roads were poor and the way dangerous. Only fools would travel by night!

But the traveller merely looked down his long nose at them. 'We follow a star,' he told them. 'We saw it rise many days ago and we have followed it every night since then. The star is leading us to the new-born king.'

'And what will you do when you find this king?' someone asked.

'We will pay him homage and give him the gifts we are bringing to him,' one of the travellers said.

'Gifts fit for a king? Who has ever seen a gift fit for a king?' shouted someone, and the room exploded into laughter again. But the travellers did not join in. They simply exchanged glances and began eating.

Hassan had stayed near the door, unseen, and now he crept away, back to the stables where he had tethered the travellers' camels. He checked the camels were settled then examined the saddlebags. They felt pleasantly heavy. Did they contain the gifts the traveller had spoken about, gifts fit for a king?

Excitement filled him. If he could take just one of those gifts, it would be enough to buy his freedom, and then he could go home! How much he longed to find out who of his family still lived! And how much he wanted to join his kinsfolk in revenge on the enemies who had butchered his mother and stolen him away!

Gifts Fit for a King

WITH TREMBLING FINGERS Hassan began working at the knots and seals that held the heaviest saddlebag firmly closed. So engrossed was he in his task that he did not hear the soft footfall as someone else entered the stable. He cried out in alarm as a rough hand hauled him to his feet.

'What do you think you're doing, slave?' a harsh voice demanded. Hassan found himself staring into the face of one of the men who had been questioning the travellers. 'Think you'd get here before us, did you? Well, you're wrong.'

The burly man threw Hassan to the floor and seized the saddlebag. In anger, Hassan grabbed his ankle and pulled it out from under him. The man fell with a heavy noise and a cloud of dust onto the stable floor.

'Well done!' a quiet voice murmured. 'You do take your duties seriously.'

It was one of the three lordly travellers. He smiled at Hassan approvingly before turning to the would-be thief.

'I'm sorry you've had this trouble, my friend.' And to Hassan's amazement, he reached down and helped the man to his feet. 'You didn't really think we'd leave such precious gifts out here in the stable, did you?' He laughed softly. 'No, they are several leagues down the road – with our heavily-armed servants!'

The Gambler

Hassan eased himself down beside the camel. His body was a mass of bruises where his new master had kicked him – today and yesterday and all the days since he had won him from Johab, the fat innkeeper.

A gambler, he had refused to pay for his meal. 'Pay? What do you mean pay?' and he'd spilled bone-white dice on to the inn table in front of him. 'Let's dice for the meal. You win – and I'll pay. I win, and we'll call it quits. Can't say fairer than that, can I?'

He had looked over at Hassan, hovering curiously to listen to this strange proposition. 'I need a new camel-boy,' the gambler said. 'That slave of yours will do.'

Johab had laughed, Hassan remembered sourly. Until the gambler won. Later his new master had boasted. 'It never fails,' and showed him proudly the trick dice he had used to cheat Johab. They had left in haste, taking a different route from the one the gambler had told everyone.

All the while, Hassan's new master played dice and cheated his way to free meals, free drinks, and all the comforts of inns along the caravan routes and in the towns and villages they came to. At last, they came to a vast teeming city. Here, Hassan was left with one of the gambler's friends in a village on the outskirts while his master went into the city and played his game of dice in all the inns.

Hassan was bored. Nobody to talk to but the camels. But at least he was free from the beatings. His wounds were starting to heal, even though there was never enough food for a growing lad. He was just beginning to feel safe and was hoping the gambler might have left him behind, when one day he heard the hated voice.

'Get the camels ready! We're leaving!'

His master was in a hurry, and it took several days of travel, piecing together the fragments of information he let slip, before Hassan had the whole story.

The gambler's trick dice had been spotted and he had been taken before the ruler of the city. 'Spare me!' he had begged. 'I could be useful to you! I can go everywhere and anywhere. I hear everything that's said, everything that's going on.'

And now they were travelling here, there, and everywhere, with the gambler busily gathering information for this ruler. Herod, his name was, and he and Hassan had something in common. It appeared that Herod wanted to know what had happened to the three Lordly Ones. Had they found the new-born king?

'Keep your eyes and ears open, boy!' the gambler warned him. 'We may win a prize through this!'

But Hassan wasn't at all sure that he wanted Herod to find out. After all, one king doesn't want another one in his territory. It would be dangerous. Hassan had the feeling that it might be most dangerous for the new-born baby king.

So here he was, making camp out in the desert for the gambler who was now Herod's spy. And what rankled most was that now he must never find out the end of the story of the three Lordly Ones and their search for a king. It was too dangerous.

Hassan scowled. He wished he'd been able to stay at the inn. There, it would have been quite safe to listen to the gossip. There was always news at an inn and he might even have witnessed the return of the Lordly Ones. There was a lot to be said for life at the inn, Hassan thought. He hunkered down beside the fire and prepared to sleep.

Desert hospitality

Drifting drowsily, Hassan became aware of quiet sounds in the night. He stirred and listened closely. That was the swish and soft padding of camels coming across the desert sands. At night? Could it be bandits? Honest men would not travel in darkness.

Hassan crept to the tent and quickly roused his master. The gambler appeared at the tent entrance, an imposing figure with his wicked curved scimitar unsheathed and shimmering in the faint moonlight.

The metallic jingle of camel harness came closer until shadowy figures appeared out of the darkness into the glowing circle of the campfire. Hassan's master raised his scimitar and demanded harshly: 'Friend or foe?'

Hassan heard a quiet mutter of conversation, then one camel stepped delicately forward. Its rider, muffled in a heavy cloak, said quietly, 'Friend, do not let us disturb you. We ride on.'

'I think not,' the gambler said in a dangerous voice. 'You must be weary.'

A second voice interrupted him. 'We must continue on our way. And quickly!'

'Must?' queried the gambler, interest sounding in his voice. 'There is time for a little refreshment, I'm sure.'

'Friend, we must journey on,' the first rider said, his voice rising.

Hassan was startled. For a moment, he thought he recognised the voice. Then the gambler's scimitar flashed.

'Boy, make our guests some tea!' the gambler barked and aimed a kick at him. Hassan dodged back into the shadows to obey but saw dimly three travellers dismounting from their camels and following the gambler into the tent.

Hassan scrambled to boil water on the little fire and brew the sweet mint tea of the desert. When it was ready, he carried it into the tent on a little brass tray, offering it on bended knee to each man in turn.

'Thank you, boy,' a voice said, drawing Hassan's startled eyes to the traveller's face. He *had* recognised the voice! It was one of the three Lordly Ones who had been following the star in search of the king. But now there was something different about him. He was no longer so lordly, so haughty...

A sharp kick caught him. 'What are you staring at?' the gambler snarled. 'Get out!'

Hassan hurried out of the way, trying to smooth the recognition from his features. He must not betray the Lordly Ones to his master. If he guessed who they were, they would not leave the tent alive.

As Hassan pulled the tent flap closed behind him, he saw the gambler emptying his trick dice out of their velvet bag and invite the travellers to while the time away with a game.

The biter bit

OUTSIDE, HASSAN KNELT by the fire, thinking hard. These men with his master were the three who had come to the inn. But now they were returning home again, and secretly. In a hurry. And his master was certainly going to cheat them – just as he had cheated Johab. He would also use the game to probe for information, information that would put their lives and the life of the new-born king at risk.

Hassan crept back to the tent and listened, peering through the tiny gap at the entrance. The dice game was beginning. What could he do?

A gleam of light showed Hassan where his master had placed his scimitar – and it was almost within his reach! Holding his breath, he reached his hand beneath the tent flap and slid it towards the scimitar, his eyes never leaving his master's face.

Just as his fingers reached the handle, a hand closed on his wrist like the strike of a snake. 'That is not the way,' the voice he had recognised murmured in his ear. 'Be patient!'

The hand dropped from his and he sank to his knees outside the tent, trembling. He could hear the brittle click as the dice were rolled. Unable to keep away, he huddled close to the entrance flap of the tent, his eyes fixed on the dice game.

The final roll of the bones on the table was followed by silence. The end of the game. Hassan waited for his master's characteristic bellow of triumphant laughter. But it did not come. Instead, the gambler was spluttering out his outraged surprise. He had been bested!

'How did you do that?' he spluttered. 'You must be magicians!'

The three travellers began to laugh. 'No, no! We are not magicians. Merely mathematicians! It was easy for us to see that you were cheating. But let that pass. We thank you for the refreshments and must now be on our way.'

They rose in dignified silence, bowed to their astonished host, and then bent to leave the tent. Outside, they stood gazing into the night sky for a moment, reading the heavens as wayfarers do. Then they turned towards their camels.

Hassan couldn't bear to let them leave without hearing the end of their story. With his master at a safe distance inside the tent where he could not overhear them, Hassan crept towards the travellers and whispered, 'Please, did you find the king? Did you see him?'

Three pairs of dark eyes turned to stare at him. The Lordly Ones had gone very still and Hassan felt an undercurrent of wariness and tension. Suddenly he felt very afraid. Did they think *he* was Herod's spy?

Hassan gets his answer

'WHAT IS IT to you, boy?' one of the travellers demanded. 'Why do you ask? Has someone told you to find out?'

Hassan swallowed hard. He wanted to run away but even more than that, he wanted to know the answer.

'Nobody told me. Believe me! *He's* in Herod's pay but I'm not! I just wanted to know... I won't tell him, I promise.' His voice cracked with earnestness. 'You see, I was at the inn – before he took me away.' Hassan jerked his head back towards the gambler's tent. 'He cheated my master, Johab the innkeeper, just like he was going to do to you.'

'Ah yes,' one of the travellers murmured. 'I remember. The camel-boy at the inn who tried to save our gifts from a thief. I knew I'd seen you before.'

Hassan was embarrassed to be reminded of what had not been an honourable episode. He hurried on. 'I heard what you said – at the inn – about the king and following the star... and ever since, I've been wondering. Did you find him? Did you give him your gifts? I just wanted to know.' His voice trailed off.

'Boy!'

It was the gambler, who appeared from inside the tent. Recovered from the shock of his defeat by the three travellers, he was now in a towering rage – a rage that looked as if it was going to be taken out on Hassan.

The gambler reached out a long arm and hauled Hassan towards him, the other already bunched into a fist for the inevitable beating. Hassan cringed and tried to double up to protect himself, waiting for the blow with his eyes closed.

A jingle of coins. The blow did not come, and finally Hassan felt brave enough to open his eyes. One of the travellers was holding the gambler's velvet purse. He was emptying the contents into the palm of his hand and holding them up so the gambler could see – a heap of gold coins and the trick dice.

'Let the boy go,' the traveller said, 'and you can have your purse back.' He held out his hand.

The gambler stared at him, then at the purse and the coins. With a swift movement, he flung Hassan away from him and grabbed for the purse. But the traveller was too quick for him. Coins and purse disappeared from sight as he pulled his hand back. Then, with the other, he propelled Hassan backwards towards the other two travellers who drew him to safety.

The gambler confronted the traveller, breathing heavily. 'A bargain is a bargain!' he snarled.

The traveller stepped back, away from him. 'But of course, my friend. You've honoured your side of the bargain and now we'll honour ours.'

He opened his hand. 'Here is your purse.' He handed it over. 'And your coins.' The gambler seized them from him and poured them back into the velvet bag.

In a swift movement, the traveller raised his arm and swung it in a wide arc, hurling the dice as far as they could go into the desert night.

'I really don't think I should give those back to you,' he said. 'It just wouldn't be right.'

He turned and spoke a word to his companions and then the three travellers were racing to their waiting camels. They mounted and pulled on the reins. The camels heaved to their feet and prepared to leave. Hassan grabbed his poor bundle of possessions and climbed on to the back of the baggage camel. Then they were away, racing across the desert by the light of the moon.

It was several leagues along the way before they let up the hard pace. One of the travellers fell back to see how Hassan was faring.

'No, I'm not tired,' he protested. 'It's very... exciting.'

'Ah, to be young,' the traveller laughed.

'Would you tell me now,' Hassan began hesitantly, 'about the king and what happened and everything?'

'It's a long story,' the traveller said, 'but we have a long journey ahead of us, so maybe there's time.' And so he began...

If *you* want to know the story of the new-born king, you'll find it in the Bible, in Matthew, Chapter 1 from verse 18 to Chapter 2 verse 12.

14. Balthazar's Feast

'Nice man, that King Herod.'
'Certainly treated us well.'
'Fancy palace he's got.'

The three travellers rode in silence again, their camels padding softly over the desert sands.

'He was very helpful.'

'Yes, though I was surprised he didn't know already.'

'Mmm. With all those learned men round him...'

'Not to mention all those books...'

'Oh well, probably doesn't matter.'

The camels' long legs ate up the miles, and the travellers passed villages and vineyards, humble homes and farms, and always the star shone brightly before them.

'There's an inn. How about a little refreshment?'

'That's all you ever think about, Balthazar!' the others mocked him.

'I'm hungry!' he insisted.

'Okay! Okay!'

The others reined in their camels and dismounted. They knew they would get no peace till Balthazar was suitably fed once again.

'Would you look at that!' Balthazar stood at the entrance of the inn, his face filled with horror. It was packed to bursting point with people.

'Hey, landlord!' Balthazar's strong voice rang out. 'What's all this?'

'You foreign or something?' the landlord answered in a surly voice. 'It's the census. Them Romans counting the people again, to get their poll-tax off them.'

Balthazar sighed and turned back to his companions.

'Now what?'

'You want a drink?' the landlord asked. 'A meal?'

Balthazar's eyes brightened up at the words.

'No chance,' the landlord continued. He waved his hand at the crowds. 'No room.' He shrugged.

'No room?' Balthazar repeated. 'Whoever heard of an inn with no room?' He raised his voice and commanded the landlord, 'Then you'd better make room!'

'Listen, buddy,' the landlord told him in a weary voice. 'The last folk who needed room, I had to put in the stable. With the animals. You want to eat your food there?'

'Come on, Balthazar, let's make tracks.'

Balthazar sighed. The stew smelled good and it looked like there were nice big dumplings in it.

'Come on,' his friends repeated, and sadly, he turned and followed them out into the courtyard again.

'Where are the camels?' he asked.

'In the stable, I suppose.'

Still grieving his missed supper, Balthazar ambled towards the stable and flung open the door. The occupants looked up in surprise – a girl, a man, and in a manger, a tiny baby.

The girl smiled. 'Have you come to see the baby?' she asked.

Balthazar stared. Suddenly he remembered his mission.

'We seek a King!' he announced in ringing tones.

The girl simply lifted the child from the manger and held him for Balthazar to see.

'He is called Jesus,' she said, and Balthazar found himself turning and running into the courtyard, yelling to his friends at the top of his voice, 'I have found him! I have found the King!'

And he knew, without even looking up to check that the star had stopped overhead, that it was true.

15. Homeward Bound

Footsore, the camels grunt,
nostrils flaring disdainfully,
as we turn them to the road again.
My bones protest –
old bones accustomed to an easy chair
and much dreaming over books.
No adventurer I –
yet here I am.
Or rather here I've been.
As my camel jolts along the road,
I ponder where I have been,
who and what I've seen.
A moment's brightness in a long life,
now left behind?
How black the night without that blazing star!
And melancholy's frosty fingers
creep around my heart.
The camel stumbles.

(We travel by night to avoid the king.)
I turn to gaze at the sky – black, so black.
But no – a million stars sparkle.
A million lights fill the heavens.
How many candles will be lit, I wonder,
at that Light we left behind in Bethlehem?
Enough to fill the night sky?
Enough to light this dark world?
And within I feel the tiny flame,
lit as I knelt by the manger,
flare into life.
And the answer comes:
'Enough. My light is enough for you.
My light is enough for the world.'
What was my gift
Compared to His?

16. Rumours of Angels

THE GREEN WAS in darkness. The houses surrounding it quiet. I'd heard a noise – a muntjac probably – but it had disturbed my sleep. I went to the window and looked out. A frosty night with twinkling stars. And a glow in the branches of the oak tree.

As I looked, it resolved itself into a human shape – with wings – that slipped down from the branches, finger on its lips, the other hand beckoning me. I could hear a clear tenor voice saying, 'Come!'

And quite without realising what I was doing, I had put on my dressing gown and slippers, hurried downstairs, opened the door and stepped outside on to the path in front of the house.

The angel stood, waiting for me. Now I'm not really too sure what I think about angels. They're not part of the chilly Calvinist theology I was brought up in – except of course for those that turn up specifically in the Bible: Gabriel so busy at Christmas, Michael and his warrior angels, seraphim around God's throne.

As I say, I'm not sure what I think about angels but it's hard to deny them when one stands right in front of you, all shiny and scary-beautiful.

'Hello,' I said.

Yes, I know. Pretty feeble and foolish. I think it/he/the angel smiled.

'Come,' he said.

I thought he meant to the top of the Green so I stepped forward. He took my hand and then it was like the Snowman film and I was *above* the Green, *above* the town, and it was as if all the Christmas lights had been switched on. Suddenly all over the town, I could see dancing lights, here little clusters of light, there bright single lights, and some that were pale and weak yet still bravely shining. But some houses and buildings had no lights. They sat in darkness.

'Do you see?' the angel asked me. 'Love – Light – shining all around you. And the darkness will never put it out.'

I looked for my friends' houses – and yes, I was glad to see that there were lights.

'And the ones without lights?' I asked.

The angel was returning me gently to my front door.

'That's what Christmas is for,' he said. 'Share the Light.'

17. Another Christmas on the Green

❖

CHRISTMAS EVE ON the Green and all was quiet – except for Horace the hedgehog snuffling his way into one of the gardens. In the middle of the Green under the big oak tree, Lola the muntjac nibbled the grass, tears in her eyes.

She looked up at the sky longingly. Was that a shooting star or could she see Santa's present-laden sleigh whizzing along, pulled by its magnificent reindeer?

She pawed the ground unhappily. How she wanted to be one of Santa's reindeer! But she was stuck here in England, a muntjac – and nobody loved a muntjac.

Far from China, her native land, her ancestors brought here at the whim of rich men and then discarded, she and her kind were now deemed a nuisance – an invasive alien species – unwelcome immigrants – having to forage wherever they could to find food.

But even muntjacs dream and Lola gazed into the velvet night sky with her beautiful eyes.

Plop! An untidy tangle of – was that wings? Some kind of bird seemed to have fallen out of the tree. Lola nosed it gently and to her amazement it unrolled into… a rather messy angel. More like the old fairy for the top of the Christmas tree – the one from years ago that has languished at the bottom of the decorations box and got ragged and crumpled and dirty.

Fred the wonky angel picked himself up and grinned lopsidedly at Lola.

'Thank you,' he said. 'Happy Christmas.'

But another big tear dropped from Lola's eyes and splashed on the ground. Horace the hedgehog who had come to see what was happening scuttled hastily to one side to miss the threatened shower.

'She's miserable,' he told Fred.

Daisy the cat came out of her hiding-place. 'She wants to be one of Santa's reindeer,' she sniffed. 'As if!'

Fred raised a wonky eyebrow.

'Well, you must admit it wouldn't really work,' Daisy said. 'You need matching reindeer to pull Santa's sleigh and a little muntjac like Lola just wouldn't fit in.'

Lola sniffed miserably. She had to admit Daisy was right.

'Yes,' Fred the wonky angel agreed. 'But maybe that's not the most important thing – fitting in.' He looked round the puzzled faces of the animals. 'Being like all the rest, I mean – just another identical reindeer. Is that really so wonderful?' he asked.

'Well, she hasn't a hope of anything wonderful,' Daisy remarked cattily.

'No?' Fred asked. 'Why do you think I'm here, visiting her?'

Daisy looked cross but Horace the hedgehog chuckled deep in his throat.

'Christmas is when we remember that everyone is so special that God's own Son came to Earth on a wonderful mission.' Fred grinned at Lola. 'I'm part of that mission and my job today is to tell you, little muntjac, that there's something better than one glamorous night's work for Santa Claus.'

Lola the little muntjac opened her eyes wide in amazement.

Fred the wonky angel did a little dance of joy. 'He told me to tell you he loves you – every one of you, muntjacs and hedgehogs and cats and people, everybody – 100 per cent, forevermore. Happy Christmas!'

And there was a spluttery untidy starburst and a garbled sound of singing and then the night was quiet and the wonky angel had vanished.

'Humph,' Daisy the cat said disdainfully, but as she stalked away, there was a smile of her lips. '100 per cent? Forevermore? Well, I never.'

18. Here Be Dragons

❈

THE SUMMER STORM had blown itself out while I slept and now morning, damp and bruised, woke me. I padded round the house making sure there was no damage, then remembered the room in the attic. I hadn't been up there for ages. It was my winter study, cosy under the roof, but far too hot in the heat of summer. Well, that's my excuse.

I pulled down the aluminium ladder and creaked my way up the flimsy rungs. The fluffy insulation between the joists suffocated all sound as I stepped noiselessly onto the boards and pushed open the door.

There on the floor, fast asleep, was a dragon. He lay, catlike, with his huge head resting on his front legs. His long tail curled behind my desk. And as he slept, he snored. Male. Obviously.

I looked up. The window was closed. The sloping eaves were intact. I stared. There was a dragon on the floor of my study. How had he got in?

With the lightning.

The answer came directly into my brain, the way music on a good stereo in the car appears exactly midway between your ears. His voice was deep and velvety.

He opened a lazy eye at me. Golden with emerald flashes. Then closed it again.

'Excuse me,' I began.

The eye opened again, less friendly this time.

Yes?

'You said "With the lightning"?'

The tail twitched irritably.

Last night's storm. He spoke slowly, as to an idiot. *There was lightning. I used it as a conduit. So I am here.* The eye closed again.

So that's how I came to have a dragon as a house-guest. He was actually a very easy guest. He would pop out when there was a storm and find himself a meal. I imagine the local farmer thought there was one of those urban-fantasy great cats out there.

There is.

'I beg your pardon?' Talking to me when I spoke out loud was one thing but listening in to my thoughts...

There is a small panther on the loose but she won't bother the local farmers for a while. The dragon preened. *I think I gave her a bit of a fright.*

'I'll bet.'

Sarcasm does not become you. The voice in my head which rebuked me changed to a light tenor, and before my eyes, the dragon vanished in a sudden gleam of sunshine from the window, and there in his place stood a unicorn. Dazzling white, dust motes dancing around him in the shaft of sunlight.

'Oh purlease!' I said. 'I'm no virgin princess! I've never been a princess and never will be. And I haven't been a virgin for many years though I admit I might as well have been these past few years!'

The unicorn shook its head, its big soft eyes sad. The sunshine went out with a pop and a dark cloud heavy with rain slid like a blind over the window. In the dim light of the study, the space where the unicorn had been was occupied by a shaggy grey wolfhound.

Well now, darlin', would that be more the thing? enquired an amused voice with a strong Irish accent.

I raised my eyes to the heavens. The hound took that for acquiescence and came over for a sniff.

I gave in and petted him. 'You're a fine beast,' I said, running my hands through rough fur which changed in my fingers to soft feathers as the hound disappeared and in my hands was a white dove.

Open the window, a soft voice cooed in my head.

Obediently, I raised an arm and opened the skylight. Off the bird flew, like Noah's dove from the ark.

My study felt empty now that my magic menagerie had left. So I did what every writer does when the emptiness hits. I made myself a coffee. I paced a bit. Straightened books and papers. Then opened up my laptop and let the words drain out of my fingers.

Later, I rose to switch on the light as the dark bulk of cloud blotted out the sun, but as I looked, I saw it was no cloud but a dragon passing by. He turned his head and winked. I waved and went back to my desk.

Moral: Every writer needs to check their study/notebook/laptop every day for dragons, unicorns, Irish wolfhounds and doves. That's where they hang out.

19. Once Upon a Parking Space

From: 'R. Collington' Collington@Accounts
To: all.staff@AmbitIndustries.co.uk
Subject: D496KYB
For the last three days, this car has been parked in my parking space. I have worked for this firm for 20 years and have parked my car in the same space for every one of those years. I must ask the owner of this vehicle to find another place to park.

From: SR@Marketing
To: Collington@Accounts
Dear Mr Collington,
I think you're wonderful too. I lie awake at night dreaming of you.
D496 KYB

To: SR@ Marketing
From: 'R. Collington' Collington@Accounts
Dear Madam,
Kindly do not add insolence to injury. I shall be obliged if you would move your car from my parking space.

To: Collington@Accounts
From: SR@Marketing
Dear Rex,
I wouldn't upset you for the world. You are in my thoughts, day and night.
D496 KYB

To: SR@Marketing
From: 'R. Collington' Collington@Accounts
Madam,
This nonsense must stop forthwith! If you have not vacated my parking space on Monday, I shall be obliged to take this matter further.
RC

To: Collington@Accounts
From: SR@Marketing
Dearest,
So heated over a parking space! There are 1200 of them in the Ambit Industries car park, not one of them reserved. Surely this car park is big enough for both of us? So what if I get up earlier and got there first?
D496 KYB

To: SR@Marketing
From: 'R. Collington' Collington@Accounts
Madam,
You cheated. I arrived early this morning to park my car in my space and what do I find? You had the audacity simply to leave your car in the space all weekend. Ambit Industries do not provide long term staff parking. I shall take this matter up with higher authority.

To: Collington@Accounts
From: SR@Marketing
Rex,
You misunderstand. My mother took ill on Friday and I was called away suddenly. I did check with Security that it was all right to leave my car in the car park.
D496 KYB

To: SR@Marketing
From: 'R. Collington' Collington@Accounts
I am sorry to hear about your mother. I hope things are improved.

To: Collington@Accounts
From: SR@Marketing
Dear Rex,
Thank you, but no. Mother died, and the funeral is on Wednesday.
D496 KYB

To: SR@Marketing
From: 'R. Collington' Collington@Accounts
May I offer my sincere sympathies? My own mother died last year so I do understand what you're going through.

To: Collington@Accounts
From: SR@Marketing
Dear Rex,
Thank you. It is tough. Any chance of a sympathy drink when I get back on Thursday?
D496 KYB

To: SR@Marketing
From: 'R. Collington' Collington@ Accounts
Thank you for your invitation. I regret I am otherwise engaged on Thursday evening.

To: Collington@Accounts
From: SR@Marketing
OK, how about Friday?

To: SR@Marketing
From: 'R. Collington' Collington@Accounts
Madam,
I do not wish this correspondence to continue. It must be terminated immediately.

To: Collington@Accounts
From: SR@Marketing
Chicken. Meet you by my car next Friday after work.
I'll buy you a drink at the Antelope.
D496 KYB, remember?

To: SR@Marketing
From: 'R. Collington' Collington@ Accounts
I'm sure you realise that my presence in the car park on Friday evening was purely fortuitous. However, if you were to happen to be in the Antelope this evening, I should be happy to return your hospitality.

To: Collington@Accounts
From: CleverCards.com
You have an electronic birthday card from SR@Marketing.AmbitIndustries.co.uk.

To: SR@Marketing
From: 'R. Collington' Collington@Accounts
Thank you for the card! How did you know it was my birthday? And the present you sent was perfect. I've been searching everywhere for that book and couldn't find it. I wonder, would you like to have dinner with me on Friday evening at Marco's?

To: Collington@Accounts
From: SR@ Marketing
I'd love to.

To: Sophie@easyweb.co.
From: Rex@homenet.co.
Dear Sophie,
Thank you for such an enjoyable evening. It is so good to meet someone with whom I have so much in common. Hope you don't mind me e-mailing you at home? I just thought – I have two tickets for the concert you mentioned, and I wondered whether you would care to accompany me?
Rex

To: Rex@homenet.co
From: Sophie@easyweb.co
Hi Rex,
Love to. And thank you for such a super evening.

To: SR@Marketing
From: 'R. Collington' Collington@Accounts
Sophie,
Just a thought. If we get a take-away after work on Friday, we could be in Manchester by 8 and catch the concert. You could leave your car in 'our' space…
Rex

20. MacAllister's Party: a story for Burns Night

✣

My heart sank when I first met him. Big, bluff, and pseudo-Scots. He had even changed his name from Ronald to Ranald. I suppose somewhere, generations back, some of his ancestors must have come from Scotland. But the man was English, no doubt about that.

Still, he greeted me like a long-lost cousin. 'A fellow Scot – that's grand!' he declared, struggling to round out his vowels. Since he was to be my boss, the new Bursar at Musa Balewa University, I kept my tongue between my teeth. But the torture continued. Every day at coffee time, he would hove into view, red-faced and sweating, to lean against the filing cabinet in the staffroom 'for a blether'. In five years, he never did manage the 'r'.

He was not a bad boss and soon brought order into the chaotic bureaucracy of the small Nigerian university. And his wife adored him. A tiny Malaysian half his age – or less – gossip hinted he had found her in a bar in the Far East. An attack of far-from-home male menopause and he was hooked, so it was said, and she was on easy street for the rest of her life. Frankly, it seemed like a good relationship to me, though I sometimes thought I detected a trace of insecurity in him – as though he wasn't sure of his ability to live up to her rose-tinted view of him, or worse, that he might one day lose her.

We were used to the occasional unusual liaison among the senior staff. One of the Nigerians would marry a long-legged beauty from amongst the students. A taciturn British expatriate would become enamoured of a girl from the town brothels. Young volunteers from Australia or Canada fell in love with bright Nigerian departmental secretaries. We were a strange mix of nationalities, the academic nomads of the world.

Generally, though, the senior staff population was solidly married and very traditional. Most of the professors were white and their wives formed a tight-knit clique which dispensed afternoon tea and approval in their cool shuttered drawing-rooms. When word got round that MacAllister had ditched a middle-aged wife back in England after he met Lee, lips were pursed in disapproval, husbands were drawn closer on their invisible chains, and ranks closed. Lee MacAllister received no invitation to afternoon tea. Dinner parties given by the great and the good were not graced by the MacAllisters' presence. In short, they were ostracised.

MacAllister's staff were in a difficult position. Already part of the university community, much was at stake, and friendships and social acceptance hung in the balance. One by one, the senior staff were picked off by the professorial wives – the men at dinner parties, the wives over the Earl Grey.

Murmured enquiries were followed by rapier-sharp interrogation as they sifted each of us for our loyalties: to them and the Establishment, or – heaven forbid! – to MacAllister.

Any hint of sympathy was censured.

'Such a bad example, taking up with a girl like that!'

'Not the thing.'
'Lowering standards.'
'Jolly bad form.'
'Should never have been appointed.'

The questions I faced often probed the nationality issue. One stern Scottish matron pronounced, 'That silly name, Ranald! Complete fraud! Who does he think we are to be taken in by that nonsense? He's no Scotsman!'

Meanwhile, Ranald and Lee MacAllister seemed blissfully unaware of their isolation or the machinations of the professorial coterie.

From time to time, MacAllister would announce they were having a party, to which a mix of other University outcasts and some of his senior staff were invited. Characteristically, their parties broke the unwritten rules of expatriate entertaining. Instead of the lavish days-of-the-Raj supper served by white-uniformed flunkies, Lee MacAllister would give her cook and household staff the night off and see to everything herself.

'She enjoys it,' MacAllister would say simply.

I remember one night after a sudden storm had disrupted the electricity and there was no power for cooking or light, Lee provided a superb banquet of exotic Malaysian dishes, cooked course by course over a Primus stove. And the meal was served by Lee herself, with silent oriental grace.

MacAllister would splash whisky into hobnail tumblers and his '*Slainte*!' would get louder and more slurred as the night wore on. At last, an unseen signal would pass from Lee to her husband, and he would lumber to his feet and remind us brusquely that we had an early start in the morning. We would hurry away, guiltily wondering which of their professorial neighbours might have seen us.

I had no idea how old he was, late 50s, perhaps. His hair was silvered at the temples, and the skin was the ageless, reddened hide of the long-term whisky-drinking expatriate. The whisper went round that soon he would be retiring. 60 was plenty old enough after a life in the tropics. The professorial wives fell on the news with joy, and relief. Having Ranald and Lee MacAllister in their midst was too much of a threat not only to their sense of propriety but also to their peace of mind. Many a husband had been caught gazing in admiration at Lee's smooth golden profile and miniature perfection, before glancing with distaste at a waist-thickened, rhinoceros-hided wife.

End of term came and Convocation, the wonderfully elaborate graduation ceremonies. As I joined the long queue for my place in the tented auditorium, I was startled by a familiar but totally incongruous noise. Could it really be bagpipes? I turned and searched around till I discovered where they were. There, dressed in starched grey shorts and blouses, was a Nigerian police pipe band. And in the perfect circle of pipers was a huge man with the big drum. Little tartan fliers decorated grey socks on smooth brown legs, and tartan ribbons circled grey berets on tight curled black hair. Not the kind of pipe band I was used to, but they knew how to play. I was enchanted.

'Grand, isn't it? A real taste of home!' the loud voice broke into my pleasure. 'Nothing like the pipes, eh?' Ranald MacAllister stood at my elbow, head nodding in approximate agreement with the music.

'Yes, indeed,' I agreed. 'What do you think, Mrs MacAllister?'

'I have never heard this music before. And it is the native music of my husband's homeland? How wonderful it is! So strong, so warlike...' Her eyes glowed and she clutched

MacAllister's arm even more tightly, gazing up at him in adoration, then back in wonder at the pipers.

A few months later I received a summons to MacAllister's office. He was pacing up and down.

'Take a seat,' he directed with a frown, then paced some more, his face getting redder and more worried. He swung round to stand in front of me.

'You remember that pipe band at Convocation?'

'Yes?'

'My wife's hired them, for a party.'

I must have gawped at him in amazement.

He launched into explanation. 'It's my birthday next week. 60. I'll be retiring at the end of the year. My wife wants to give one last party and now she wants to make it proper Scottish style, with dancing… and haggis … and…'

My eyebrows went up even further.

'You know, like a Burns Supper,' he snapped. 'Like a damn fool, I told her about them. Part of the culture, you know? So now she wants to have a Burns Supper, for me, for our last party here.'

'I'm sorry,' I said, feeling rather uncomfortable. 'I don't quite see…'

'I want you to organise it for me. The party's on Tuesday. Today's Thursday so you've got plenty of time.'

I started to argue but his voice steamrollered over my protests.

'We'll talk about it again tomorrow, when you've had a chance to think about it. What preparations are needed, the stuff for the haggis, that sort of thing, okay?' and he showed me out.

It was a masterly piece of force majeure. But there was a problem. I wasn't the Burns Supper type. I vaguely recalled one as an undergraduate at University that I couldn't get out of, but that was about the sum total of my knowledge.

In the Staff Club that night, over the fried chicken and yam chips, I discovered there was more to this Burns Supper than met the eye. It was the general opinion that MacAllister was about to get his come-uppance – at the unsuspecting hands of his adoring wife.

MacAllister, it was believed, would be quite unable to produce a genuine Burns Supper and in the ensuing debacle would lose face before the whole community, and before his wife. To add to the piquancy of the joke, he would therefore probably lose the wife as well.

'Serve him right, a man of his age. He should have known better' was the general consensus.

At work the next day, MacAllister called me once again into his office.

'Well,' he barked. 'Have you thought about it?'

'Yes, Mr MacAllister,' I began. 'The trouble is, I don't really know all that much about Burns Suppers so I don't think....'

He went bright red as he stared at me, the veins standing out on his shiny forehead.

'What do you mean?' he demanded, leaning threateningly over his desk at me.

'I'm not the best person to ask. Organising Burns Suppers really isn't my cup of tea,' I began apologetically. I started to explain my predicament but it was lost in a torrent of words.

'Damn it, you've got to do it! Who else can I ask? The thing is, well, damn it, my wife expects me to manage the whole thing. She's hired the pipe band, told Tomas our cook to await my instructions about the food. But, but...' Here he swallowed hard. 'The thing is... You simply must help me! I haven't a clue how to go about it! I've never been to… Of course, I've read about Burns Suppers, but I've never…'

He was really struggling now. 'So, I thought…' His eyes turned pleadingly to me. 'I wondered if you … as a great favour… if you would…er…organise the whole thing for me? Discreetly, you understand, so my wife will not know…?'

I did understand. Perfectly. But how could I tell him that I really did not know how to organise a Burns Supper either?

He lurched towards me, his hands outstretched.

'Please say you will! You know how these things are done.' He paused and gulped, then added, 'After all…you're a real Scot.'

All the bluff posturing was gone and in its place was a badly worried man. I took a deep breath and hoping I would not regret my decision, said the only thing I could: 'I'll do my best, Mr MacAllister.'

He seized my hand and wrung it wetly. 'I knew I could rely on you!' Relief shone amidst the perspiration.

I hurried back to my own office to think. What had I let myself in for? Head in hands, I gazed unseeing at the blank wall opposite as I racked my brains. Haggis. How do you make haggis? I had no idea, but we had a good library on the campus. Maybe I would find some help there.

'Bless you, Isabella!' I murmured as I returned Mrs Beeton's famous tome to the shelves. I had copied out the recipe and made a shopping list for the MacAllisters' cook.

I knew that the traditional accompaniments to haggis were 'bashed neeps and champit tatties' but neither potatoes nor swede grew in Nigeria. They were not imported either. Our local potato substitute was yam but it made a heavy white fibrous mass. Thoroughly mashed and with plenty of butter and milk added, it might do. And the addition of puréed carrots to another batch of yam would provide some neep-like colour. Add nutmeg and plenty of pepper and maybe we could disguise the blandness of the yam.

I reckoned we might be able to get away with it. Considering the limitations we were working under, no one could expect MacAllister to produce the real McCoy. He had plenty of good whisky to help wash it all down. That would certainly help the cover-up!

I moved along to the poetry shelves in search of Robert Burns. With a Scottish Head of the English Literature Department, I was sure to find a selection. My confidence was not misplaced. But as I copied out the 'Address to the Haggis', my apprehension began to grow. MacAllister would never get his Sassenach tongue round Burns' glorious Lallans. I would just have to coach the man and leave him to do his worst.

By Monday lunchtime, we were both in tears. Mine were frustration, MacAllister's were rage and defeat. He had struggled, yet again, through the first three verses. It was a mangled wreck of the poem and he knew it. Although I would be one of the few 'real Scots' present, it still would not do.

He took a deep hopeless breath and plunged on:
'Then horn for horn, they stretch an' strive:
Deil tak the hindmost, on they drive,
Till a' their well-sweeled…
weel-swelled…
swalled…
kytes be …'

He broke off. 'I can't do it! I just can't. "Weel-swalled kytes belive!" It's beyond me! And while we're at it, I don't think I'll be able to stomach that damn haggis either. It sounds disgusting. Yeeugh!' he cried, his voice rising to a crescendo of horror and despair.

I stared at him, my mind racing. We had to have the 'Address to the Haggis' but maybe that did not have to be MacAllister's party piece. Maybe I could do that. But he had given me an idea. Quite forgetting myself, I clapped him on the shoulder.

'Don't worry about it. Tell you what: *I'll* do it. What *you* can do...' and the afternoon passed in a much lighter mood, though I worked MacAllister just as hard.

Then it was Tuesday night. The sky was a velvet blanket hung with Christmas lights. Cicadas creaked and in the darkness was the thrumming of the ever-present drums from the nearby village.

As the guests arrived, cars were parked on the road so the wide gravelled drive in front of the house remained clear for the dancing. Indoors a U-shape of tables, covered with starchy white linen, filled the dining room. There were tartan streamers everywhere – where Lee had found them, I'll never know.

The pipe band slouched beside the kitchen door, shadowy figures in the darkness. MacAllister introduced me briefly to the pipe major, who towered huge above me.

'You'll take your instructions from her, okay?' Then MacAllister scuttled indoors, muttering something about getting changed.

The pipe major was a huge black Hausaman, his grey police uniform a pale ghost in the night. I explained about piping in the haggis. He nodded, a tall slow man of few words.

'Madame, I know of this.'

Anxiously I stumbled on.

'Do not fear,' he interrupted me gently. 'All will be done correctly' and he turned and left me.

I went into the kitchen, blazing with fluorescent light and rich with the smells of spices and cooking. On the kitchen table was a huge platter, heaped to its rim with a double ring of creamy white yam and the orange of the carrot-yam mixture. In the centre was the steaming mound of haggis.

Through the kitchen door drifted the noise of the guests, in a fever pitch of anticipation and curiosity. The bets were on that the party would be a disaster and the professorial clique had their spies in place.

A sudden shriek split the night as the piper filled his bag, then settled into a low drone as he held the pipes in readiness.

Tomas the cook lifted the platter. 'Now, madame?'

'Now.'

We made a strange procession: the tall piper in his grey uniform leading the way, then Tomas, in his best kitchen whites, proudly bearing the haggis shoulder-high, and lastly myself, barefoot in flip-flops under a long skirt made of a thin cotton plaid I'd found in the local market.

As we marched to the top table, the skirl of the pipes swept away all conversation, banishing the heavy breathing of the African night, and conjuring in its place Celtic melancholy and Celtic pride.

MacAllister waited at the top table, in a kilt. Lee MacAllister beside him shimmered in a silver cheongsam.

Tomas laid the platter before them and stepped aside. The piper cut the music into sudden silence, and I fumbled in my skirt pocket for my carefully typed copy of the 'Address to the Haggis'.

'Fair fa' your honest sonsie face,
great chieftain o' the puddin'-race!
Aboon them a' ye tak your place…'

A glance round showed me a rapt audience. On I went, gesturing at the 'groaning trencher', the 'hurdies' and the 'distilling dews'. Into the next verse and time to grab the big carving knife. I brandished it and plunged on:

'His knife see rustic Labour dight,
an' cut ye up wi' ready slight.'
Into the haggis went the big knife. The contents spilled out and drew a satisfying 'Ah!' from the guests.

At last, the poem was over. The piper and Tomas retired to the kitchen where the pipe band was to be fed. I circled the table and sat down in my place while a scurry of servants served plates of haggis and the ersatz 'neeps and tatties' to the guests.

MacAllister lifted his fork and dug in, his bluff joviality more than a little fixed. I recalled his apprehension about the haggis and held my breath, watching him intently. I prayed he wouldn't let us down now.

His Adam's apple bobbed as he swallowed. Slowly the taut muscles of his face relaxed. He scooped up another forkful, then another. Then he seized his whisky glass and threw back a large mouthful. Red flooded his face and a broad smile. He gazed round the room at his guests tucking in contentedly, and nodded, well pleased.

Lee MacAllister, I noticed, took tiny birdlike pecks at the food on her plate, her eyes ever turning to her husband. As he relaxed and beamed, a small smile of pleasure touched her perfect profile. MacAllister patted her hand affectionately.

'Grand, just grand,' he told her and filled his glass again.

Replete and content, we left the debris of the dining-room and moved out on to the veranda, set with armchairs and coffee tables. The night's coolness welcomed us.

'Now to the dancing!' MacAllister announced in a loud voice after a brief respite, waving the energetic among the guests on to the smooth sandy drive.

The grit under the thin leather soles of my flip-flops felt incongruous. I remembered having to learn to dance during PE classes at school in the winter. I could see again the big honey-coloured floor of the hall and smell the polish, its shiny surface treacherous underfoot. The boys were lined up along one wall, acne-scarred and aggressive in false bravado. The girls, pert and saucy, pretending not to care, lined the other wall till the teacher instructed 'Take your partners!' and the scuffle for the most popular girls began. An old gramophone played scratchy records. Gratefully I remembered some of the dances: Strip the Willow, Eightsome Reel, Dashing White Sergeant.

I chose a Strip the Willow to begin with. The easiest. It took a moment or two to get everyone lined up on the drive in two sets, while the pipe major approached out of the darkness.

'Which tune will you have, madame?' he murmured.

Panic slammed into me. I had not expected this. I had just expected them to play the right tunes.

'I don't know the names of the tunes,' I whispered to him in shame.

I could see the dancers beginning to fidget. 'The best laid plans o' mice and men...' Ah well, I had done my best but now everything was ruined, gang properly agley.

I glimpsed the shimmer of Lee MacAllister's silver cheongsam. She and Ranald were standing on the veranda, watching and waiting.

A movement to my left revealed the silent spies in the next-door garden: Professor Stubbings and his tall forbidding wife, a leading light of the ostracising committee. A glance to the other side and I was sure I had seen her chief supporter, Professor Lindsay's caustic wife, behind the bushes, her timid wee husband beside her.

Everyone seemed to be watching and waiting. The moment seemed to stretch into eternity. I wanted the ground to open up at my feet and swallow me. What could I say to MacAllister? How could I let him down now?

He must have sensed something was wrong for he started down from the veranda. Then the pipe major suddenly leaned down from his great height and hummed softly in my ear.

'What about that one?' he asked.

I felt a dizzying wave of relief as I recognised it.

'Yes!' I said. 'That would be perfect!'

The pipers rallied and began their sonorous clamour. I shouted instructions to the dancers and the dancing began sedately. The couples set and turned and moved gracefully, with a few bumps and giggles and apologies. Nigerian turned with Australian, American with Hungarian, Dutch with Irish, Canadian with Polish, French with Egyptian. And then they got the measure of it and each other and demanded an encore.

The pipe major hummed another tune for my approval and we were away. The nationalities blurred as they turned and whirled and called and laughed. And from somewhere in the background, MacAllister produced a 'Heee-euch!' loud enough to wake the dead – that primitive warcry let rip at so many ceilidhs and weddings to encourage the dancers now sounding out into a Nigerian night.

The effect was startling. The dancers stopped in their tracks and applauded, roaring 'Well, done, MacAllister!' 'Good man!'

A shocked voice came from the bushes, 'That was MacAllister?' and the branches parted to bring Professor and Mrs Stubbings fully into view on one side, and Professor and Mrs Lindsay on the other.

Meanwhile the two sets had merged into one until finally the dancers collapsed laughing into their chairs where servants bought cooling drinks.

After a few moments, they were on their feet again, calling for more. This time an Eightsome Reel. We had plenty of room and enough volunteers for two sets. The non-participants ringed them round, and the music began. As the reel grew wilder, MacAllister began another blood-curdling 'Heee-euch!' but this time it was taken up from the darkness by a new voice and the glorious duet rang out on the night air.

A startled pause, then heads turned to find the source of the new voice. But MacAllister was there first. Striding down from the veranda, his hand outstretched, he bore down on wee Professor Lindsay.

'Man, that was wonderful!' he declared. 'Care for a drink?' And without a moment's hesitation he had put an arm round Professor Lindsay's shoulders and was leading him towards the house.

The Stubbings, looking on, glaring, disapproval incarnate. Mrs Lindsay remained, alone, her face tortured as she watched her husband disappear with the despised MacAllister.

As they reached the veranda, MacAllister turned.

'Hey, Mrs Lindsay! I hear you're a grand dancer. Come and show these youngsters how it's really done.'

A chorus of voices rose from the dancers: 'Join our set!' 'Come on, Mrs Lindsay, we're just starting again!'

With unerring timing, the pipers launched into a really toe-tapping tune, then as the dancers assembled again, MacAllister and Professor Lindsay 'heee-euched' in perfect accord.

Mrs Lindsay hesitated for only a moment. Amid cheers, she left the shadows and was welcomed on to the dance floor.

She turned back, for a moment, to the Stubbings. 'I don't suppose you dance, do you?' she said.

Author's Notes

❖

Here are a few explanatory, background notes about the stories and poems, in order of appearance.

'Donkey Story' was written during the years I lived and worked in Northern Nigeria, where I saw many a donkey with its colt, heavy-laden, going about its work. It was my first published short story, appearing in a South African newspaper, *The Southern Cross*, in March 1977, and was my first attempt at looking at Gospel events and wondering what happened to some of the other people in the story.

The next three – 'All That I Have', 'The Girl He Left Behind', and 'Roses Have Thorns' – follow that pattern. What did the mother of the wee boy say when he came home and told her he'd given his lunch away? Did the Prodigal Son have a girlfriend that he left behind? And wouldn't Saul/Paul have been married?

'Raedwald's Queen' was written in 2009 during a wonderful year when I was part of Suffolk Poetry Society's co-operation with the National Trust at Sutton Hoo. I was one of several designated Poets in Residence who were blessed with special access to the site to inspire our own poetry, and then were allocated a local school to spread the inspiration. There was a poetry competition for the children and I was thrilled that it was a boy from 'my' allocated school who won. And my poems were read during the special weekend event, and printed in a commemorative booklet.

Sutton Hoo is a very special place – there are lots of burial mounds, the largest being a ship burial for a high-ranking Anglo-Saxon leader, now thought to be Raedwald, king of East Anglia who died c. AD624. Just before the Second Word War, his burial mound was excavated first by local archaeologist Basil Brown, and amazing evidence of the ship and treasures buried with him were discovered – including a fabulous helmet – and the items I mention in the poem. The 2021 film, *The Dig*, gives a good impression of that time and the finds.

It is thought that Raedwald travelled to Kent where he was converted to Christianity.

'King of the Jews' is a story of another period of turmoil, both nationally and spiritually. It was inspired by the myth of St Veronica who was said to have given Jesus her veil to wipe his face on the way to Calvary.

'One more stupid war' perhaps echoes the thoughts of the heroine of the previous story, but brought up to date. I wrote it in 2007 during the war on Iraq.

'Happy Christmas, Muriel' leads into a group of stories for/about Christmas. Two – 'Happy Christmas, Muriel' and 'Practice Makes Perfect' – are modern-day stories; 'Rhyme and Reason', 'Going On Holiday?', 'Hassan and the Lordly Ones', 'Balthazar's Feast' and 'Homeward Bound' are located in and inspired by the Bible narrative of Christ's nativity. The last two in this section – 'Rumours of Angels' and 'Another Christmas on the Green' were stories I wrote to pop inside Christmas cards for my neighbours on Rectory Green in Halesworth in Suffolk.

The next two are light-hearted oddities that I thought you might enjoy. 'Here Be Dragons' was inspired by the eyrie – the wonderful loft-conversion study I had. And as to 'Once Upon a Parking Space' – I suppose the young would text these days?

Last but not least, like a matching bookend, is another story from my Nigerian days. And yes, in essence, it happened to me. My boss came in one day and instructed me to organise a Burns Supper for his birthday. His wife (not Malaysian) had hired the police band we'd seen at Convocation (University graduation ceremony). That was the grain of grit in the oyster shell. Just about everything else is fiction! I hope the result is as much fun as the actual Burns Supper was!

Dorothy Stewart
When the Boats Come Home

A Christian novel about family secrets, romance and revival.

October 1921 and the herring fishing fleet have converged on Great Yarmouth for the autumn season. Wick fisherman Robbie Ross has come to blows with his father and been thrown off the family boat. His sister, war widow, Lydia, reluctantly sets out to bring him home, little knowing her world and her family are about to be turned upside down.

Available in paperback and Kindle editions

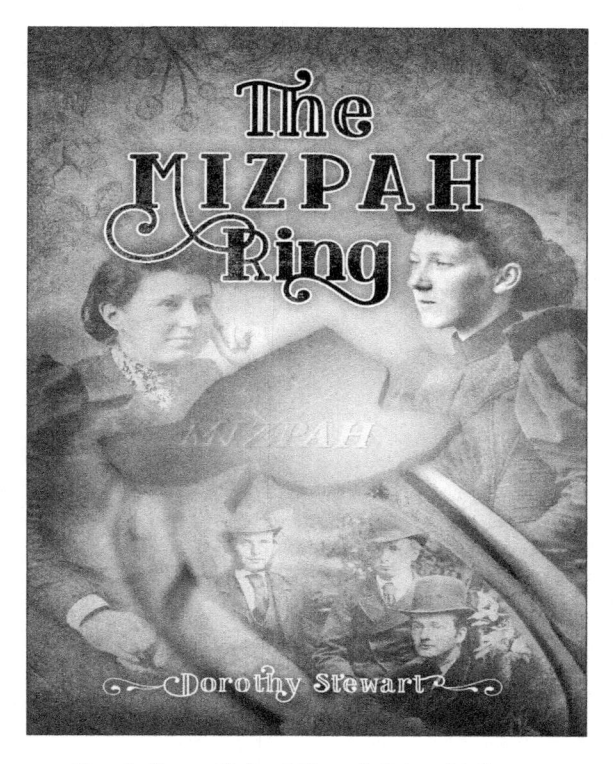

Book One of the Mizpah Ring Trilogy

'I wouldn't marry you if you were the last man on earth!'

And so Belle Reid sets in train three generations of heartbreak and sorrow, death and disaster.

Geordie, her spurned suitor, sets out from Wick to make his fortune in the Klondike gold rush of 1897 – but his ticket to that fortune depends on the rival Belle has chosen over him. When the lads find gold, and rival Hughie has the Mizpah ring made to send to Belle, it's time for Geordie to make his move – and only one of them can win.

Available in paperback and Kindle editions

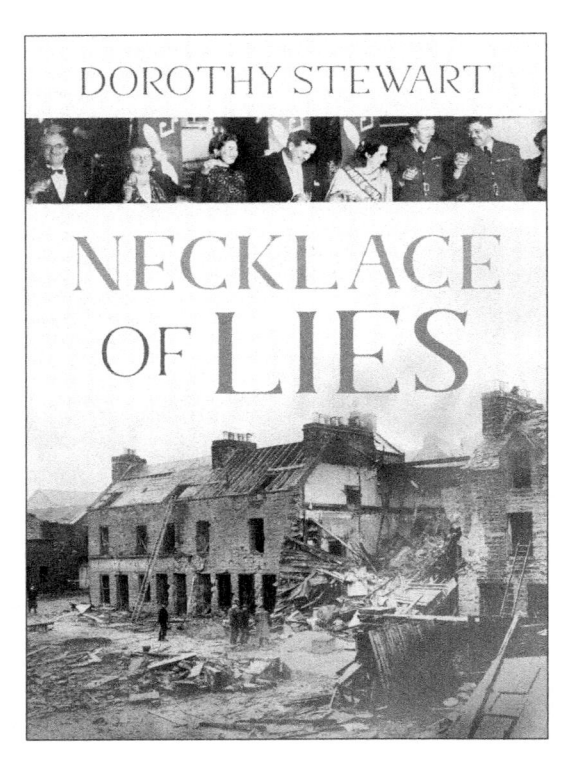

Book Two of the Mizpah Ring Trilogy

Necklace of Lies introduces the second generation of Cormacks, Mackays and St Clairs as their lives intertwine and play out against the backdrop of Wick in wartime. Must they follow in the footsteps of their parents, or can they strike out afresh and make new lives, new futures for themselves?

Available in paperback and Kindle editions

Book Three of the Mizpah Ring Trilogy

Summer of 1964 – miniskirts, the Beatles, a typhoid epidemic, and the circus comes to town. Plenty for local newspaper, Caithness Sentinel, to cover. Under new management after a recent take-over by a Canadian tycoon with new money and new ideas – and a marked aversion to the female reporter, which reopens old wounds and entangles three families once again in a web of heartbreak and potential disaster.

But must the sins of the fathers reach down to blight the lives of their children and grandchildren? Or can the third generation of Cormacks, Mackays and Sinclairs break the hold of the past?

Available in paperback and Kindle editions

Printed in Great Britain
by Amazon